Klaus Kertess is an author, curator, and art critic. His short story 'Desire by Numbers' originally appeared with Nan Goldin's photography in a 1994 Artspace volume. In addition to fiction published in *BOMB* and *Sun and Moon*, he writes art criticism for numerous journals including *Artforum*, *Art in America*, *Vogue*, and *Out*. He curated the 1995 Whitney Biennial, and lives in New York City.

D1446123

Other Mask Noir titles

SOUTH BROOKLYN CASKET COMPANY

by Klaus Kertess

SERPENT'S TAIL

HIGH RISK BOOKS

NEW YORK / LONDON

Library of Congress Catalog Card Number: 96–70954

A catalogue record for this book is available from the British Library on request

The right of Klaus Kertess to be identified as the author of this work has been asserted by him in accordance with the Copyright, Designs and Patents Act 1988.

"Footnotes," "South Brooklyn Casket Company," "Another Winter," "Short End," "Black Rainbow," and "Storm Warnings" have appeared in *Bomb* magazine. "Desire by Numbers" originally appeared in *Desire By Numbers* (Artspace) and is used by permission of the publisher.

First published in 1997 by Serpent's Tail,
4 Blackstock Mews, London N4, and
180 Varick Street, 10th floor, New York, NY10014
Website: www. serpents tail. com
Cover design by Rex Ray, San Francisco
Phototypeset by Intype, London Ltd
Printed in Great Britain by Mackays of Chatham

Contents

Saving Salvador

Part One

Headlines

New York Times, Sunday, February 24, 1980
"Salvadoran Official Killed, Rightists Are Blamed"

New York Times, Saturday, March 8, 1980
"Salvadoran Banking System is Nationalized"

Part One

Dialogue

No, Peter, it's not true. It's just not true.

Yes it is, Manolo.

Anyway, it has nothing to do with my story.

It has everything to do with you. I'd rather let the pen probe the secrets of your first sexual obsession than chronicle a class struggle. Your having been secretly in love with James Malcolm is far more compelling to me than the demise of yet another South American banana republic.

Central American. El Salvador is Central American.

Central to you, peripheral to me.

But you said you would help me. You can write, I can't. You know my country; you were there.

Yes, long ago, when we were in college, and you were secretly in love with James.

But you remember El Salvador.

What do I remember? I remember "Yho de puta" and a lot of exotic clichés, if clichés can be exotic. I remember matching sisters with matching jewels, glistening white mansions with swimming pools, flamboyant flora and fawning servants, tarantulas, your pet parrot whose lush camouflage made him all but invisible in the kaleidoscopic excess of your mother's garden, men's strong necks and women's hothouse breath, hair as smooth and black as ebony, rubies and diamonds, and guns. I remember being aware of guns for the first time in my life—a uniformed guard in an embrace with a machine gun by the gate of every house, and a heavy revolver in every glove compartment I opened. And, on the streets, I remember running into walls of hard eyes dense with resentment and envy because I wore shoes. Wearing shoes made me rich; being rich made me guilty.

But maybe you were already blinded by those clichés before you arrived. And certainly you didn't seem to mind the rich while you were there. Something you are not telling has happened since then. For years you always kept repeating what a good time you had in Salvador.

Oh yes, it was hard not to. Every night a party that was very often in my honor. Rooms that sparkled with flawless, fulgent grace, lithe limbs leading my awkward ones into a merenge or a mambo; dark, dulcet eyes and crimson-crested smiles adorning flawless skin as succulent as an orchid, Guardis and Tiepolos and Aubussons—everything twirling and unfurling in rococo swirls of abandon that knew no end. And nature seemed, there, to be just as compliant: a volcano as decoratively exhilarating as the spumes of artificial fireworks and quite content not to erupt, that tropical rain forest with its laughing waterfall, the silken sand shaded so gray on the Pacific side, the thick-skinned fruits bulging with lusty juices so surprising to one who knew only the regimentation of the supermarket's dyed oranges and pale, pasty, preripened tomatoes. How could I not have a good time? It was preordained; nothing else was possible. Even your servants seemed to think it a pleasure to wash and iron my clothes long before the fabric might dare a modest blush of dirt. And I had sex for the first time.

That was the first time?

Yes.

I don't believe it.

Unfortunately, it's true.

I remember now that it took you a long time.

Manolo, I was wildly terrified and excited. I had only indulged my body with food and swimming—my cock knew only my furtive hand, and even that but rarely. There I was belatedly living out the generic male adolescent's dream: a tropical land with a dark, low-ceilinged whorehouse that was incensed, candlelit, and blessed with the ridiculously punning name of Grotta Azzura. Her name was Linda, although she really was not. "Loma Linda." She was too young to properly minister to my foreign-tongued inexperience. I came before I entered. She had to work furiously to bring me back again— rubbing my body with her breasts and sucking my cock into reluctant hardness until I discovered myself pumping her wildly and helplessly releasing violent yells and groans that almost shattered my lonely repression. You and your cousin ran into the room with a gun and a flashlight to find me laughing and trembling in an Olympic pool of semen and sweat. She was already douching in a makeshift bidet, washing you and me out of her cunt. You had had her first. We laughed all the way to the country club bar, wondering what aberrant offspring might

3

burst from a fiery-eyed whore so nearly simultaneously impaled by a spic and a gringo.

So how could it not have been important for you to be there?

Important to my reluctant self-knowledge—sure. That constant, soothing sunniness made my body blossom for the first time. That wonderful warmth gave a weight to my balls and a volume to my cock that joyously anchored my mind to my crotch. My tongue grew to know the taste of the earth for the first time; dark tastes of musty tortillas, crumbling cornmeal, and dried, pepper-spiked beef sank deep into my glands. My mouth had only known the occasional soft seduction of French food, but, for the most part, had been anaesthetized by the culinary ineptness of a succession of my mother's maids—to say nothing of the staunch spicelessness of prep school and Yale fare. Certainly all that was new and extraordinary. With the exception of swimming in the ocean, I was not to encounter my body again until you and I ventured on our obligatory La Dolce Vita tour of Italy.

But it's all going now, the country is being destroyed—you must help me write about it.

What shall I write, Manolo? A young gentleman's guide to food and fucking in sunny Salvador, with an alphabetical listing of the cleanest bordellos and which restaurants you don't have to bring your own toilet paper to?

Why can't you be serious? Your answer to everything is "let them eat cake and cock."

Cake and/or cock. Let's give them a choice.

Oh Peter, please help me. After all, your country is largely responsible for running mine. The CIA and the Communists are taking everything away.

But Manolo, we're just a banana republic ourselves, now.

We just act out ideas of power that we once had. Our tools are bigger than yours, but just as ineffectual.

But you saw how wonderful it was. You never complained. You never sounded like a socialist while visiting Aunt Elena's coffee plantation or while trying to ride my father's polo ponies, or when borrowing the Ferrari my brother left behind.

Yes, yes, wonderful but so claustrophobic.

What do you mean?

That, when I was there, only the tarantulas seemed capable of evading your control. I never even saw a weed in anyone's garden.

Someone has to tell the story.

There is no story, it already ended before you were born. Your father is the end. Now you want a new beginning in the place you previously wanted to flee. You who spent all your time leaving—to a house in Mexico City, a lover in Honduras, and a wife in New York. The total escape that you so long and longingly dreamed of lost its lure when someone else imagined it for you, and then made it come true.

It wasn't just imagination that kidnapped my father and cut off one finger a day until they got their ransom. Every morning, a finger in a leather pouch was nailed to the wall. And then the still warm stump of his hand. The blood—the blood is still on the wall. The servants were scared to wash it off. Oh God, it was so awful, and he is so good. He built decent houses for all the plantation workers and a school for their children. Now they're burning the houses and dividing the plantations. You can't grow coffee on small plots—they know that. They're ruining everything, it's crazy. Nothing will be left. Now they're seizing the banks and paying us back in insults—worthless government bonds printed with my father's blood. They're not just looting my future, but theirs, too.

A book can't change that. If it could, how would I deal

with the claims that the wealth of your past and present grew out of the crushed backs of countless possessionless peasants?

We never stole. The land was ours.

Oh Manolo, this is hopeless. A book is hopeless. A book cannot avenge, nor reform, nor redress; it hardly knows in advance its own address.

But people will see. It would help them to see.

Only, perhaps, to see themselves. Really, why do you want this tome?

I owe it to my father.

What about getting even with your brother? Expose him one more time . . .

No—my brother doesn't matter anymore. I owe it to my father.

Part One

Narration

"And he hated his mother. And he hated his father." Peter had written that some time ago. It had given him a certain release. A release that permitted hate and love. He had never really permitted himself to hate before—nor to love.

Permitted himself or been permitted. Permission to love and permission to hate now revolved around his thoughts of Manolo. Manolo wanted a book written because he thought he loved his father. Peter had once written a book because he thought he hated his father. Did Manolo really love his father? Why did he need to ask another to bear witness to his filial rites? Was Manolo even capable of love? What was he capable of? A vast chasm of context and experience now separated two people who had once been so synchronized in their closeness.

Was it a different context or different experience that made Manolo seem so irrelevant to Peter now? Wasn't it precisely his irrelevance to Peter that made it possible for him to entertain notions of reconstituting Manolo on the page? Could he reinvent someone he still loved? No. It was far easier to steal from the past than from the present. Wasn't the violence of writing more necrophilic than murderous? How often had he resisted the verbal vortex seeking to suck the one he loved into the page— freezing come and blood in the ice of ink. What love could survive a sonnet?

Peter was a thoroughly dreamy thirteen when he had first met Manolo. An end of the school year picnic at the private school Manolo was about to enter and Peter was about to leave framed their encounter. A football field temporarily given over to the subtler combat of parents, students, and teachers. A bright sun and clear sky reflected the discreet affluence of the surrounding Protestant suburbs that had filled the school with blue-blazered, blue-eyed, stripe-tied adolescents.

Peter had almost no role in this mask of WASP well-being. His half-inward gaze had been pulled forward to be mesmerized by a group slightly removed from the predominating throng of blond and brunette rectitude. This group was animated by richer rhythms. Suppler limbs, more lustrous skin, darker hair, deeper eyes, and clothes that caressed rather than merely covered their bodies. Women in possession of and happy to adorn themselves with weighty rainbows of gems. More than willing to be wealthy. Spanish speaking. Landed Latin American oligarchs of coffee and cane whose sons were here to perfect their English and to acquire enough of the Protestant work ethic to ensure the timelessness of their wealth.

The cold, Episcopal Gothic halls of this particular school were warmed by the vapors of South American Catholicism. The school's proximity to New York City, its respectable, but not taxing, academic standards and its Christian all-whiteness, assured by the discreet racism of Protestant affluence, made the school a proper preparatory for many of the heirs of coffee and cane. Four years of a reasonable prep school, four years of a reasonable college, a year of debauchery in Paris, Geneva, or Madrid, then home to settle into a wife and mistress, child propagation, and business. The regimen of regulating plantations, corporals, and coups would then be relieved by twice-yearly trips to Paris and New York. Lives that were as regular and golden as the routine of the sun that ruled their riches.

The school was equally divided between day students and boarders; the boarders were equally divided between North and South America. It was at night that one could most clearly savor English made juicy by Spanish. Peter had been a day student, but he had always yearned for the fraternal secrets of nocturnal Spanish. The winds of reverie constantly wafted his eyes toward the looks and limbs of the South Americans—the lush language, the confident carriage, glances that danced with fire, black down-crowned testicles that descended sooner and lower than those of the others ravished a mind that was not yet firmly anchored in a body. An adolescent melancholic with a mania for Latin cultures. Years would pass before he would realize, with some shock, that this obsession was not uncommon to his parents' Germany. Now he only knew this passion as particular to himself.

A precocious interest in painting and many months of sickness had led Peter to the Italian quattrocento and his first Latin longings. His mother's countless art books brought more relief than his stern grandmother's compresses or his doctor's prescriptions. Pages of medicinal sun, revealing clear forms and finely tuned lines—high-foreheaded, columnar figures firmly and calmly rooted in regulated serenity. And artists' names

8

almost as resonant as their creations; Sandro Botticelli, Paolo Uccello, Piero della Francesca, Gentile da Fabriano, Domenico Veneziano. Their firm resilient roundness bounced on his tongue.

His father's name was Helmut. For years, Peter had only known the name as a jagged signature at the bottom of letters sent to his mother that always contained a message for him and his brother. The signature did little to explain the long years of absence that coincided with Peter's constant sickness. When words were finally proffered in explanation, they had little more substance than the signature. Perhaps, no explanation could be sufficient to fill the blank space of his fatherlessness between the ages of four and nine.

His father's absence, at this picnic, was quite simply explained by his distaste for superfluous socializing and his desire to reread the *Bhagavad Gita* over the weekend. Then, too, he would be happy to be alone with the new maid whose firm youth was such a relief from the overripeness of the Swede who had recently victimized the household with her cold efficiency.

Peter's mother's presence was as predictable as his father's absence. She was unwavering in her devotion to the notion of the family. Her maternal duties could not be deterred by the unexpected tension that arrived with her new employee. She stood in the middle of a group of local parents. Less prosaically dressed than her neighbors, she was Chanel-suited and accessorized. Her speech, however, was her most striking accessory. The accent that had been such a burden during the war and that had caused so many backs to turn was now a social asset that helped form the image of European sophisticate pressed upon her by neighbors whose tongues were still wrapped with a midwestern twang. She was undoubtedly discussing the family's impending departure for Germany and France. Happily conjuring up the joys of the Riviera to those whose affluence had not escalated as quickly as her husband's. Not mentioning her mother's five-flight walk-up apartment in a still bombed-out block of Berlin, or her brother's job as a carpenter.

For the last three years, the yearly pilgrimage to Germany had been made bearable by a two-week stay at the Hotel du Cap in Cap d'Antibes. Bikinied and goggled, Peter would ogle the spiky sea urchins that studded the subaqueous rocks, or else suavely swim out of sight in the Mediterranean's emerald embrace. In the water, the body that so often rasped with the congestion of asthma, acquired an ease of breath and self that was as yet unknown to Peter when he was rooted to land. It was no longer the time of Picasso and the Murphys, but the Côte d'Azur had not yet been pockmarked by the full democratization of the summer tour. Peter was dubbed "le dauphin" by the staff. It was 1953; Peter was thirteen.

More than even France, he now longed for the fall. Then he would go to another school. A school that necessitated his boarding there. Some place with air not thickened by parental quarrels, maternal possession, and paternal dispossession; a place hopefully spiced with Spanish. This picnic was his farewell.

He looked up to meet the beckoning call of the sister of one of his classmates. She was among the South Americans talking to someone Peter had never seen before. He was happy to heed her call. Manolo was his name. The name sounded right. He was from El Salvador. He would be a new boarder.

The school had previously known but two other Salvadorans. The first had been Ricardo Suarez, whose gaudy gregariousness outflashed the Cuban contingent that was customarily the most willing to flaunt wealth and wildness. By his senior year, Ricardo had convinced the administration that his Cadillac convertible and suite in the St. Regis Hotel were indispensable to his needs and survival. The second Salvadoran had been Manolo's slightly older brother. His compact, fierce good looks and athletic prowess had won him the nickname "Wolf." He had only stayed for a year or Peter would have known him. Manolo would be burdened with being Wolf's brother. His thin frame and gleeful indifference to discipline disappointed those who expected him to step into the legend of Wolf. Four years would elapse before the formation of Manolo's and Peter's friendship.

Part Two

Headlines

New York Times, Tuesday, March 12, 1980.
"Salvador Army Steps Up Drive Against Leftists"
"Family of Salvadoran Pays for Ad at Bidding of His Leftist Captors"

New York Times, Tuesday, March 25, 1980.
"Salvador Archbishop Assassinated by Sniper While Officiating at Mass"

Part Two

Dialogue

Why can't you believe it?
I can believe it; but I can't make it believable.
Please, Peter, it's you I counted on for the truth.
I could only bring a rhythm to your anger.
Why not the truth?
There is none.

You must believe in the truth of something.

Desire.

Desire, desire, desire—that's all you ever talk about.

That's all that we share besides death.

So your pen becomes a penis.

No. Absolutely not. The pen is, and the penis is. One shrivels at the touch of the other.

We're not getting anywhere.

You're right, Manolo. Why not just let the *New York Times* solve El Salvador? You've got the front page now—the archbishop's assassination caused a media meteor. Months will pass before El Salvador burns itself out in the forgetfulness of the back pages. Maybe several years; maybe Salvador will acquire enough momentum to become more memorable than Uganda or Namibia or Ethiopia or Afghanistan or any of the countless surfaces of the earth roiled by violence. But perhaps to be forgotten would be the best.

I can't forget—how can I forget my country?

As long as I've known you, you've tried to forget your country. You wanted to inherit your share but not live in it.

It's not true, it's just not true. I hardly left the country for three years, I worked at the bank every day of the week. I went over the coffee accounts, with Father, on weekends. I only went to Paris once and only twice to my house in Bahia . . .

Maybe I just knew an earlier manifestation of you. Three years ago you would still have thought a comintern was a bird, now you're obsessed with the Communist threat.

And you—you only mock the world or toy with boys. That Greek that slipped by as I arrived seemed young enough to get you into legal trouble.

No; but in another year, he will be past his prime. Admit it, you thought he was beautiful, too. Too beautiful, of course. And those bedeviled eyes that it seems only Greeks are permitted to have; and his so flooded with the bittersweet curse of his perfection.

Is your florid praise camouflaging incompletion?

No, the couch's freshly clotted velvet can attest to that, but I came more in a dream than out of desire. I hardly know whether it was while embedded in his roseate asshole or while sucking his rigid root. More masturbatory than mutual, such beauty triggers more fantasy than fulfillment. It could have happened without me touching him at all. Mainly I remember the mirth of his marble mouth as he stood in the doorway extending a single red rose to my enthrallment. As absurdly obvious as it was satisfying. Opening my door will never be the same again.

See, there you go again. All you understand is clichés. And how much time was required to arrange his arrival?

Much more than I care to recount; but, sometimes, the pleasures of shopping outweigh the meal.

So you harness all your energy to such transient pleasures?

Yes, I diddle while Rome burns.

Oh Peter, I don't believe you.

We seem to have trouble believing each other.

You never seemed so uncommitted before.

You never asked me to keep score in your civil war before.

You call it keeping score, when half my cousins have been kidnapped and killed?

They don't add up to an archbishop—or do they?

What about Miguel Alvarado? You said you wept for days when you heard they stuck needles in his eyes and let his horse drag him home at the end of a rope around his neck. His son has been mute ever since he found his battered body by the gate.

My tears couldn't wash away the want and rage that

killed him. I knew Miguel as a strong and gentle friend; his killers knew him as a conspicuous symbol of the wealth that froze them in social and economic immobility. I hated them when they killed him, but my hatred could take no form.

Your words are so cold. Miguel never harmed a soul.

But certainly his position did.

So you think the guerrillas are right?

Right, wrong; right, left. I can't see a side; I only see waves of carnage that can't be parted into right and wrong sides. Conspicuous consumerism now seems more obsessed with combat arms than cars. Newspapers compete to chart the hit parade of bombs and bombers, handguns and snipers. A man of minor intelligence can now assemble a missile on 42nd Street and launch his celebrity from a rowboat in the Hudson River. The assassin's path is the shortest route to stardom. Murder and media have coupled in a dance more delirious than any invented in those already obsolete discos. Some point to the CIA as the dance instructor, others have merely grown deaf and numb from the music's manic volume.

And you, you're quite happy to be a sardonic wallflower.

Who said I was happy? I'm just waiting for a different dance.

I remember you ten years ago when you were politically active.

Not active, outraged. For six months, I turned over my outrage to the shrill rituals of politics. Maybe I helped, in some minuscule way to end the war in Vietnam; but mostly I stumbled in and out of the minefields of white liberal guilt. If you want to aggravate the scabs of those old wounds, you'll hear numbing chants supporting your other side. "Hands off El Salvador. No more Vietnams," I'll vainly shout.

But that's not true.

Maybe not, but it could easily become my voice.

So you take my brother's side.

Your brother could be more believable. Sympathy more readily sides with the underdog and that makes him seem real. Your brother bequeathed the better part of his birthright to his peasants and insists the rest of you do the same. He could be the new Zapata, while you must remain the rich oppressor. Then there is the twist that he is gay.

So you would make a religion out of his homosexuality?

No. Religion without the lie—a region. You and he and I all live in that region. But he is pursuing power and politics, while the popularly perceived role for homosexuals plays itself out in the realm of style. He dares beyond the decorative. When was the last time we had a gay hero?

You're worse than that real estate heiress that let herself be fooled by him.

Fooled into love . . .

No. Fooled into a big donation to his Democratic Revolutionary Front. Oklahoma real estate contributing to Communist land redistribution. You don't think that's ludicrous?

No more ludicrous than your father attending mass after the assassination of the archbishop.

He didn't kill the archbishop.

Who did?

Extremists no one can control.

But someone must support and supply.

Not my father.

So the guilt for the war is just to be painted on one side.

Oh Peter, you won't listen. Did that woman deafen you with my brother's propaganda? I know she's your friend, but everyone says she's as crazy as she's wealthy.

Very capricious maybe, but not crazy. Actually, she is extraordinary.

You say she loved him, but he couldn't have loved her—he's never loved a woman.

How do we know? They say I loved her once, too.

Oh God—first you want him to be a homosexual hero, then you have him falling in love with this lunatic heiress.

It makes a better story.

Did she tell you lots of stories about him?

No, none really.

She must have said something.

Only how wonderful he was. "Fantastic" was the word. "So fantastic," she exhilarated over and over again. "So fantastic."

Part Two

Narration

By night, a swan with an opal body and ruby eyes crowned the comb that seemed to ride rather than restrain the languid waves of her blond hair. Whether the flush that flickered across her fair skin was the reflection of the swan or the breath of a more urgent inner flame remained uncertain to those around her and to herself as well. By day, opalescence was banned; her hair was reigned by stark pins that forged the form of a twisted bun on the nape of her neck. Her skin remained constant in its milkiness; her full lips only occasionally betrayed her cool composure with an unwanted twitch or, more seldom, a softly flickering smile. The swan was replaced by the frozen fire of a single flawless diamond of some seven carats, at the end of an all but invisible platinum chain—chain and stone so finely attuned to her flesh and bone that the diamond's fire appeared to be permanently embedded in the cleft of her clavicle (a location that detoured the eye's path to the soft crests of her breasts). Body and being hid behind this cold burning that even hindered contact with the nearly black depths of her almond-shaped eyes, preventing them from revealing the secrets of the night. Like many a nocturnal flower, she spent the day in pristine closure, awaiting nightfall to unfurl her fragrance and her form.

Her diurnal and nocturnal manifestations filled much of Peter's life for almost three years, first as friend, then as lover, and finally as acquaintance with the occasional rights of lover and friend. Theirs had not been a passionate love so much as a union that served mutual tastes, desires, and fears. They shared experiences rather than creating them together. They acted out a love for fear of not being loved—a fear rooted in what each imagined to be a loveless childhood. He and she were joined by that anxious familiarity disoriented travelers extend to each other when they discover their passports have the same covers. They indulged in a delay of destination for the temporary comfort of community. Theirs was a community not of desire for each other so much as for a still unknown other. Primarily, their relationship tranquilized the gnawing anxiety of waiting for the liberating arrival of the other. The secret desire that united them was as absurdly simple as it was complex and intense. Each was obsessed by the mournful yearning for a certain male, Latin type. Neither the erect grace of the Classic Greek nor the fierce and false pride of an Augustan Roman aroused their desire. Refinement was not a prerequisite for their complement; something more earthbound they required—a figure carved from a chunky block, firm but fluctuating to flaccid, square of hand and foot, a chin capable of command, eyelids hewn like helmets and hovering over deep brown orbs, a mouth of fruity fullness barely contained by the crisp clarity of its contour and ever ready to slide into a near lascivious smile; muscles as willing to ripple firmly as to roll softly, a resilient garland of flesh wrapped around the waist and dissolving into the firm hemisphere of the stomach, hung with bulky balls and a corpulent cock restless to become stiff. Independently, they had arrived at an identical list of features that each held secret from the other. Their longed-for type was one rarely favored by artists but had, nonetheless, obsessed Caravaggio and modeled for the dissolute side of the Divine seen in the Davids of Donatello and Michelangelo. Such a type, with sufficient grace to counteract natural coarseness and sufficient intelligence to balance brazenness, each fervently sought. The abundant, youthful sensuousness of Mediterranean or Caribbean persuasion found in New York, could easily (more easily for him than for her) provide a palliative for the loneliness of the night but had yet to fulfill the ruthless requirements of his or her fantasy.

How many bars had he cruised, how many boys lured home, only to find himself more sated than fulfilled? How many months, how many years went by before he began to question the benefits of his persistent prowling, before he realized that what he prayed for very often turned him into prey? How many limp dicks, how many watches, radios, cameras, and cufflinks disappeared through his door? How many cases of gonorrhea and crabs and sheerest boredom? How many mornings did he awake to the abrasive ring of unrequited vulgarity? How many tricks before he felt tricked? How long before the rarity of the fabulous fuck threatened to erase even the shallowest illusions?

He still did not know. He still did not find incredible the possibility of perfection waiting to step out of the dark dankness of some sleazy bar and into the light of his proffered smile. If he was not in love, he had to stay in shape by being in love with the idea of being in love. Was his identity so fragile that every encounter became definitive? Were there others who anticipated more than an anonymous speedy ejaculation? What were they wishing there, in the waterfront bars? The executive who traded his tie for a chain, his embarrassed "straight" friend caught with his pants down and his cock up; a former fling, once reluctant, now recumbent in a trough and beaming up at the one-eyed squint of a mammoth black cock; the well-known museum director lasciviously leering through a smothering cloak of apprehension; the ubiquitous French tourists with brittle asses and a smugness that made them blind to Peter's taunting gaze (did the French ever do more than masturbate?); the Puerto Rican hustlers whose flickering fingers thrilled more to the feel of leather wallets than of skin; the lurching college student racing to pass out before his prayer for penetration would be answered. He thought he knew them all, he thought he knew their wishes. Stereotypes all of them, but what stereotype was he? Were their desires really less urgent than his own?

He exercised his persistence not just in bars designed for his and others' longings but also in buses, subways, restaurants, airplanes, cocktail parties, movie theaters, beaches, supermarkets, elevators, his dentist's office, and the street. The less familiar the place, the more brazen he became. He, who for so long hid his body in a hunch and hooded his brow with a frown, whose physicality was so long hidden to all but his hand—who would have guessed that his sexuality would so insistently seduce his psyche? He, of course, would be the last to know.

And she, was his partner similarly preoccupied? Yes, but, perforce, more subtly so. She could not so readily dissolve in the anonymity of a bar nor sally forth in street pursuits. She who knew mainly the lonely expanse of her limousine would be too completely disarmed in the frantic glare of public transportation; and shopping she hardly did in public. Except for an occasional farmers' market in the country and her yearly appearance at the Paris couture, almost all was delivered to her door—including her suitors and assignations. Her townhouse was indeed more town than house; although too chaotic to be called a salon, it was, nonetheless, inhabited and visited by some of the best minds and bodies of the decade. The immensity of her wealth was lure enough; but her grace, her intelligence, and, above all, her determined enthusiasm, made her bait all but irresistible. If her fervor frequently turned to irresponsibility, it only aided in eroding the barriers created by the seriousness of her fortune. Caprice erased threat. Her enlightened restlessness succeeded in spreading her pleasure. She might totally exhaust a piano teacher for two months so that she could quite competently play all the works of her favorite new composer, only to disappear to Idaho to photograph rocks, after talking most of the night with a geologist at the birthday party of her best friend, whom she completely ignored. She could forget to mail her annual pledge to a choreographer dependent upon her support and then make up for it with a lavish party in his honor. She could spend two days on the phone finding someone to bring Jacques Derrida to dinner, after attending one of his lectures and becoming enthralled with the complex waywardness of his crossword puzzle mentality. But then she would get distracted and flabbergast the philosopher by seating him next to a lugubrious lifeguard in need of some mental musculature. She was always obsessed but her obsessiveness was constantly shifting its shape and substance, seeking succor as readily in the sublime as in the banal. Was it choice or surrender that formed her failure to frame a life that was more than extravagantly picturesque? The dreamed-of Latin lover was the only constant in her life.

Already she had been married twice. The first time to a deservedly unknown journalist whose main function was as an agent of separation from her family, although he did father her only child. The second husband was closer to her dream—a Chilean architect of moderate means and radical political persuasion. While capable of the proper rage and occasional passion, he was no match for the dream. As servility began to overtake this husband's mien, she hastened to reclaim her maiden name. She left him a sizable bank account; he left her a poolhouse in the shape of a snail.

After the second divorce, she yielded completely to the reign of her restlessness. She fluttered from male to male, silently and playfully pollinating her fantasy. In all her couplings and uncouplings, she found protection in an almost obsolete, virginal helplessness that bestowed upon her partner an intoxicating illusion of strength. She always seemed more the sister than the seducer. The first febrile touch of her long fingers sought safety more than flesh. Surely, it was inadvertence that permitted her fingers to stray to the inside of a thigh or brush against the tip of the crotch en route to the grasp of the other's hand. And when her body began to slowly arch in languor, it seemed more in response to fatigue than to desire. So softly she would collapse into her partner's embrace. And when they were finally in bed, it surely seemed that only her partner's mastery was responsible for caressing her reluctance into full sensual compliance. And then modesty, even consternation would take its turn; and the suitor had no choice but retreat, seldom if ever to return. A few, a very few, played extended engagements, only to find themselves left with nothing but the alleged guilt of taking sanctuary in her name.

Ariel. She was born an Ariel among Peggy Sues, Sue Annes, and Janes; a de Rocheline amongst Hunters, Hodges, Shermans, and Thompsons. Perhaps, it was the elaborate shelter of the name that encouraged the formation of a being so exotic and quixotic. Ariel de Rocheline certainly was a name that permitted one to engage in extravagances more readily than those more mundanely named might dare—just as the baroque phantasmagoria of coral bodies provides protection for certain species of fish, making it possible for these favored fish to assume a jeweled translucence not practical in the drabber depths where such opulence could only please their predators. Long before she became it, her name cordoned off and colored a terrain inviolably hers.

The vast fortune seemingly so necessary to the name was claimed by her father who was a dour but diligent son of minor peasant nobility. He left his native Normandy for the simple reason that there were already too many brothers employed by the family's dairy. He emigrated to Oklahoma at the behest of a distant cousin who promised to put his accounting skills to good use in the offices of an oil concern. The year was 1922. As much as he was capable of being overwhelmed, he was overwhelmed by the vastness of the West and Southwest. His awe was translated into obsession; his modest career advances were marked by the acquisition of parcels of land in Arizona and California that seemed quite undesirable to more American Americans. Neither rich nor poor enough to be seriously threatened by the depression, he watched his book of deeds grow thicker right through the 1930s. At the time of Ariel's birth, acquisition had already turned to development: houses as dry as the Arizona air and as determined as the sparse vegetation had begun to sprout and multiply in apparent violation of the desert's want. Pools, golf carts, and ranch houses roamed over vast oases of consoling mediocrity.

What the father acquired the mother quickly mobilized into the mandates of empire. Jeanine de Rocheline scraped the drabness from her husband's diligence and replaced it with the shining armor of style. While her husband's houses multiplied toward an anonymous infinity, she oversaw the erection of the one structure that could be identified as solely that of the de Rochelines. Starting with Frank Lloyd Wright and Le Corbusier, she gave audiences to every major architect of her age. She finally bestowed the privilege on Mies van der Rohe, after dissuading him of his customary glass and steel in favor of brick. Forthwith she commissioned Miro, Masson, Matisse, and Leger to design tapestries for the vast tunnel of her entrance hall. Her zeal grew with her husband's wealth; her beauty, her humor, and her light touch easily veiled the harder edges of fanaticism. She knew just how to make charming her husband's newfound enthusiasm for Coca-Cola and how to be entertained by the unabashedly banal container of ketchup that seemed to cause her Baccarat crystal to shudder.

Although her manner was as new to her as her husband's wealth, it clung to her as effortlessly as the rippling pleats of her countless Fortuny gowns that so many people assumed she was born in. The beauty of her three daughters was only to be expected, as would be their culture and grace. Not to be expected was the return of Jeanine's long-suppressed impetuousness in the increasingly chaotic life of her oldest child, Ariel.

Jeanine's pre-de Rocheline life was little known but avidly and frequently speculated upon. One could not be French, intelligent, and beautiful in Oklahoma City without encouraging a great deal of speculation. Matisse and Brancusi were hardly household names there, but they took on new meaning when they both were found to have done affectionately inscribed drawings of a languidly nude Jeanine. She did freely admit to two previous marriages, one at the command of her father, one at the command of her heart. But only a very few knew that she had no money and had been brought to Oklahoma from Paris by a cantankerous dowager who found her too diverting to leave behind. Oklahoma did not boast a large French population, so it was all but inevitable that Jeanine and de Rocheline should meet.

Just so, it was all but inevitable that Peter and Ariel should meet. They were blessed and burdened by the same age, the same friends, and the same passions. They had everything in common but what they wanted the most. They were almost as fully formed as life was to permit; they still had every right to deem themselves desirable—at least ten more years would have to pass before the democracy of the flesh would be openly deposed by the dictatorship of decay. She charmed him; he pleased her. As ambivalent as his sexuality was at the time, he found nothing but comfort around her; he had no illusions about the identity and role of seducer. Although their union threatened perfection to those around them, it was only to survive in his fiction. Like so many others, he would take her name in vain.

Part Three

Headlines

New York Times, Wednesday July 9, 1980
"U.S. Loses Ground in Central America and Backs Changes in a Bid to Recoup"

New York Times, Thursday, August 14, 1980
"Salvador's Leftists Call General Strike"

Part Three

Dialogue

Have you ever noticed how many dykes drive Datsuns and Toyotas and have their plates stamped with the likes of "T Dance," "Tennis 4," and "Jog 2"?

24

Months have passed since we have spoken and all you can open with is lesbian licenses.

Really more like the monograms of the mainstream middle class than license. License . . .

Oh Peter, please don't try to lure me into a web of puns. Why are you always so defensive and cynical?

Do you really want to know?

Of course.

To sidetrack your meaningfulness.

What do you mean?

To delay the inevitable sameness of our conversations. To subvert Salvador instead of saving it, because I can't believe in your loss beyond the level of our personal friendship.

You call it "personal" when a whole country is being destroyed by evil?

Upheaval more than evil—*Flowers of Upheaval*, maybe that could be the title of your book.

Stop. Don't start again. Your country is responsible. Your country that has made a religion out of private property claims to be in league with justice while defiling the very premise the nation was built upon. It is your Carter who has taken our land away for redistribution and has nationalized our banks. Think how he would whine and whimper if some foreign power forced the appropriation of his paltry peanut farm. What about your poor migrant workers? Why not give them Jimmy's peanut farm? What about all your poor blacks? Or, why don't you give some of the land around your own house to one of those migrant workers in Bridgehampton?

Don't mention blacks. They're not even permitted to cross your borders.

What do you mean? Who told you that?

It's true, isn't it?

Well, yes, it's true; but we didn't make that law.

Your "we" has a remarkable way of retracting.

What do you mean?

I mean that you shed responsibility for your generals and colonels when an archbishop is assassinated. Your justice, like ours, is one-sided.

How can you who moments ago denied the existence of evil presume to use "justice"? And what about all the guerrillas' victims? What about their torturing and kidnapping? Is that just upheaval? Is my brother's side the only one permitted to kill? What does he want? He took our land. What's left?

The army. The officers that wouldn't let Duarte take office in 1972, but installed Colonel Molina instead, replacing ballots with bullets.

But then they invited Duarte and the Christian Democrats to join the government.

Yes, seven years later. Their invitation was made out of desperation to forestall further defections to the Left.

So the Democratic Revolutionary Front has more rights than we do?

They seem more believable. Your brother saved his birthright by surrendering it.

No. The Communists will get rid of him as soon as they have used him up.

Maybe.

Is that all you can say, "Maybe"?

Maybe.

Oh, Peter . . .

Look, Manolo, I'm sorry. Neither you nor I have very much to believe in. Your brother does. You are furious because your lifestyle has been disrupted, but you have no real belief.

How do you know what I believe in or what my brother believes in? Why is he so pure? Couldn't he just be taking revenge against our father? You, you're just romanticizing a false revolutionary. You trust the propaganda in your papers more than you trust me. The rich are always wrong, aren't they?

I wish they were.

That's not an answer. You never answer, you always evade. Evasion. Evasion. Evasion.

Calm down. Can't we talk about something else?

What else? How happy you are in debauchery?

Come on, I'm neither happy nor debauched.

No boys today?

Not today, not yesterday. What makes you think that all I do is boy toying?

It's all you like to talk about.

No, not true.

Well, so much for that conversation. Now what?

Now, who is being defensive?

All right, I know—let's talk about believing. Tell me, again, what you believe in.

A few friends, a few cocks, a few painters, a few writers.

That's a lot for you.

Not really, some fall into more than one category.

And so you try to dissect their desires and pin them to your pages in passive orgies of Proustian analysis.

No, not really. Analysis seems to have exhausted belief.

Do I hear you renouncing your Proust?

No. Proust already knew the futility of analysis. He turned analysis inside out; he mocked conclusion. Proust brought language to a halt, not to a conclusion. Analysis was merely the solution that dissolved the substance of words into an infinitely languid intricacy of surface. The surface was self-sufficient—an endless train of moments on its way to the edge of emptiness.

Thanks. Now you're offering me a ticket to nowhere.

Not me, Proust.

And you?

I haven't achieved Proust's persistence. He took to bed, surrendered his body to his pen and transformed his blood into ink. He is the true Christ of writing.

So your transubstantiation takes the reverse route; you wish your pen into a penis.

No, no. I've already denied that. Art is more androgynous; it has no tolerance for such purely phallic figures.

So it's hermaphrodites you are looking for?

Now, who is the mocking one?

Me, yes, but you are impossible to talk to. Every time we speak our conversation gets shorter.

Shall we try another topic?

What's left?

Your brother. Don't we always end up with your brother? Let's start with him. Have you seen him recently?

No. You're provoking me again. How could I have seen my brother? Why are you always asking about him?

He is here again, isn't he?

You think he calls me? If he is here, it's to raise money and spread lies. He's already taken my money, so why would he call me?

He is your brother.

He's not my brother anymore.

Part Three

Narration

Alone, lonely, lonesome. How many times had he indulged himself in writing those words? In being them? How many sentences, how many paragraphs, how many chapters had been ordered to fall in line behind the lieutenants Alone, Lonely, and

Lonesome? All three were now marshaled to march in rhythm to the roll of the ocean. He savored the spray released by the words and surrendered to their accumulating mist. Aimlessly, he meandered down the beach, now kicking up drifts of sand, now bending over to pick up and savor the smooth frosting of a shard of glass, now setting his eyes loose in the rumpled, satiny sheen of the ocean's pre-sunset surface; now resisting the urge to crown his closely-shorn head with the empty shell of a horseshoe crab, now scanning the dunes in search of his dog. His dog moved as aimlessly as he, but at a speed so wild that it implied a purpose. He darted up and down the dunes in a mad zigzag, stopping only occasionally to chew up a skate egg case or sniff a dead fish. His gait was as tireless as it was elegant. Bred to track lions in a pack, he now had to satisfy himself with tugging at the shaggy mane of an occasional sheepdog. His diffidence had made him all but impossible to train beyond housebreaking; but, somehow, he and Peter seemed always to end their wanderings in the same spot at the same time. The dog knew nothing of the variations of loneliness that preoccupied Peter.

Loneliness had so constantly been a tenant of Peter's consciousness that he simply assumed its ubiquity. In actual fact, he had not been alone at all—this being one of the few hours in several weeks that found him without a partner. But the idea of loneliness shielded him from a vague malaise that was not customary to his usual summer composure.

Summer was his time. His tastes were summer tastes— from the intensity of its sun to the extravagances of its herbs and spices. Summer's mirror provided his body with a fuller, firmer reflection than the one he encountered in the winter. In the winter, no amount of discipline could prevent his shoulders from hunching over; and, try as he might, he could not imprint his cock on his jeans (it required more time than most bars

29

permitted to discern the willingness in his crotch). In the cold, his face and hands were his most apparent features; they emerged independently from his lifeless layers of clothes; others looked draped, he always felt shrouded. It was only the lushness of his lips that was capable of the promise of physicality. Fingers of elongated but firm grace paid constant obeisance to those lips with offerings of nicotine and alcohol. Summer put his mouth in proper proportion and opened out his body. The ocean stretched and straightened his shoulders into a surprising broadness and brought forward a substantial chest over his flat stomach. Winter's asceticism was shed; and long, lean legs and arms unfurled their rediscovered life in the limitlessness of the ocean.

But this summer, he was to turn forty and found himself obsessed with the process of aging. In spite of good health and not infrequent flattery, he mused drearily and disturbingly on his own decay. Had he been sick he might have been more focused; but, as it was, his affliction barely succeeded in frustrating his productivity with a constantly nagging negativity. Two root canal operations and the need for reading glasses had precipitated his latest bout of self-indulgence. His former pleasure in his reflection was now replaced with a tarnished misgiving. He sucked his stomach in lest he be mocked by the looking glass. He hurried through his morning toilet for fear of being trapped in the tedium of yet another inventory of wrinkles. His discovery of a small congregation of stretch marks on his ass led him to seek out the more prominent marks of age tattooed on the older denizens of the beach. His eyes traversed valleys of curdling flesh and lost themselves in marbled mazes of varicose veins. Could proper exercise have retarded such collapse? Should he go to the gym, should he drink less, should he be wearing looser bathing suits? Was he becoming repellent to the younger men he took such pleasure in cruising? Would his smile betray the strange envy he felt for their smoother flesh and firmer muscles? Was his vanity propelling him into the clichés of an aging gay?

The joust between boredom and euphoria that had so often grazed and graced blank pages was now increasingly being won by boredom. He had barely managed a few notes based on the cohorts of his mother's Florida widowhood before becoming embarrassed by the bathos of his subject. The morning hours that had once been ruled by his pen now disappeared in vapid clouds of melancholy. He dissolved all substance but could resolve no surface. For the first time, his unease could yield no product. Quite often, he simply set himself afloat in the currents of an erection. The last month had been spent in a cavalcade of random couplings and near affairs that seldom survived the second day of idling on the beach in drably obligatory afterplay. The solicitations of near strangers that began to clog his telephone brought more fragmentation than completion. If only they had all evaporated in his ejaculations. Some ten years had passed since he had had sex so indiscriminately; but then it had been charged with the tension and excitement of doing it for the first time, at a moment when homosexuals were going public with a vengeance and jubilantly proclaiming their place in the avant-garde of the sexual revolution. Now listlessness filled the rings once occupied by that sensual circus. His current sexual encounters were hardly more efficient at killing time and diverting depression than solitaire or masturbation.

Memories of his recent promiscuity vacillated between a smile and a manic fidget of embarrassment. It had started with a local hairdresser. Peter was driving past the entrance to the gay beach when his eyes locked with those of a wiry jogger. Why not stop the car? In spite of his sweat-drenched clothes, the jogger reeked of some class-for-trash cologne and was equipped with a vial of mouth spray. A smooth, hairless body and a long thin cock that was readily aroused quickly landed both in the hairdresser's bed. His house was filled with pillows, prints, and figurines of frogs that were accompanied with pleas to say, "Please," followed by "talk dirty and fuck me." The cologne and the frogs left more impressions than the hairdresser. They never even exchanged names.

Then there was Tyrone the houseboy whose black feline grace had outlasted a variety of careers from dancer to decorator to servant. Within minutes of approvingly smiling at each other, at one of the local gay bars, Tyrone had taken Peter's non-smoking hand and placed it inside his pants; but at home, he proved to be much slower. He tortured Peter with an hour of his life story to the tunes of Mabel Mercer, before quickly undressing him, sucking his balls and ass while whipping his cock into an orgasm, and then passing out under the mournful gaze of his employer's bull terrier.

And Frank the semisuccessful theater producer. He was squat and quite unattractive but almost compensated for his physical shortcomings with the gusto of his absurdity. With more glee than certainty, he provided Peter with black silk socks and garters and rubber suction cups for his nipples before sucking his socked toes and his cock in endless rounds of amyl nitrate-induced hyperventilation. Peter might even have seen him again were it not for the discomfort caused by the discovery that his former analyst was spending his vacation performing in a summer stock production under Frank's aegis.

And, and, and. There were many more, too many more. Grumblings and gropings, whisperings of "piss on me," the occasional anxiety of an erratic erection, the request to do it with his fist—faceless cocks and asses barely capable of providing punctuation marks for his boredom. His wistful smile spoke more of the regret, rather than the wisdom, acquired in the shedding of most of his illusions. One encounter, however, did imprint his sheets with something more than semen. A French actor once treasured by Pasolini and Bertolucci for his angelic beauty but now somewhat bruised by middle age and the frustrations of concocting science fiction in an alien tongue. Parisian narcissism, no matter how elegantly engaging, had previously proved to be a repellent pole to Peter's erotic magnet; but, suddenly he found himself pulled into a strong embrace with this thin aquiline beauty still marked with an angel's name, if not mien. Gabriel. Happily, he began to don the armor of amorous oblivion to feel protected, for the first time in months, from the scrapes and scars of social engagements and professional duties. Aflush with adulation, Peter threw himself into the present. Only the insistent regularity of his stomach motivated him out of the horizontality of beach and bed and into his kitchen to cook his best. But soon the oblivion began to crack. Gabriel began making nervous phone calls in his native tongue, assuming Peter could not understand or, perhaps, hoping he could. In any event, the speaker on the other end had money while Gabriel clearly had none. He was lying about his absence to the other end. Peter quickly realized that unless he made a bid, all this would end. He refused. One day, he left Gabriel on the beach to go sailing with some friends. Gabriel mocked and pouted as Peter departed for the first and last time. Peter had lost or gained four days; he didn't know which. Slowly Gabriel's features melted into the rubble of Peter's amorphous melancholy. His fingertips soon lost their feeling for the silken softness of Gabriel's hair.

Peter had now turned around to walk back down the beach to his car. His resolve to let down the anchor of work and to put an end to his wayward drifting was simultaneously formed and forgotten as he abruptly noticed a seated figure, at the entrance to the beach, who was steadfastly staring in his direction. At him or at his dog or at the torrid orange of the sinking sun? Even as he drew closer, the stranger's need to squint against the flaming sun hid the goal of his stare's true target. His elusive gaze was set in firmness. His chest bristled with black curls and muscles that could well have been molded in a medieval warrior's breastplate—only the hard ochre protuberance of his nipples belied a military purpose. Muscular efficiency extended through his arms and legs—not the artificial trophies of a bodybuilder, but sinew and tissue acquired in some more natural endeavor. Square palms stretched into resilience by boldly formed fingers, toes like curved bullets. The steely straightness of his nose might have wounded his face with pride were it not for the lavishness of his lips. His lips that slowly rolled into a smile while his eyes remained still hidden in the wrinkles of his squint. He had the tenacity of those plants hardy enough to survive by the side of the sea. The target of Peter's own stare was unmistakable; but he had no idea of his stare's duration. Who was this man? He must have a name immediately.

Leandro. Unconscious of his bluntness, Peter simply asked for the name, as he sat down next to him and let the hairs on his bare right leg softly graze and tickle those on Leandro's left leg. Leandro now turned out of the sun and let his eyes open fully into Peter's, but with a look too inscrutable to fathom. Peter fell into the uncustomary grip of shyness; he was not uncomfortable. He knew this person; somewhere, they had sat at the ocean's edge like this before. When? Where? Why did Leandro seem so familiar? Why was Peter's hand so stubbornly refusing to reach for the firm fruit bulging in Leandro's crotch? Having been this bold, why couldn't he proceed?

"Why is your hand not on my cock?" Rich, Spanish-spiced English. Peter erupted into laughter; Leandro laughed. Peter rolled over on top of Leandro and kissed him until Leandro started biting his lower lip so hard he had to withdraw. Immediately, Leandro started to talk. The dog was too wild, too beautiful. Didn't Peter know how disloyal beauty was, how dark its rules, how impossible to possess? Why have a dog not capable of the proper fidelity? Was Peter a mere aesthete, some moon-struck writer or composer? The harangue rolled on, now mocking, now stern. Peter was more and more excited by the rumbling gravity of the voice; but his own tongue became as insolent as his hand had been, refusing to launch a response or even a brief riposte. He knew this was just the beginning; free of apprehension, he dared himself to be happy. Who was Leandro and why was he sitting on this beach? This was not his place. A stringy female jogged by and cast disapproving glances at two males so nearly entwined. East Hampton had a beach for every inclination; this beach was a family beach. Leandro smiled, she quickened her pace. Leandro rose, announced his departure and proclaimed that they would meet at the Attic later on, without designating a specific time. Peter stifled his penchant for punctuality and assented, somewhat anxiously. He would have to try not to torture himself with impatience. Luckily, he had been invited out for dinner.

The Attic was the slightly sleazier and looser of the Hampton's two adjacent gay bars. On weekends, it swelled with the sweaty mock frenzy of disco dancing mostly performed by couples slightly too old to still be flaunting bare-chestedness and skintight jeans. During the week, the Attic provided diversion for summer employees and a group of intrepid residents that included a few blacks claiming not to be gay but only unable to find fuckable white girls. Peter knew too many of the regulars too well. When he arrived, Leandro was, thankfully, already there, dancing with the Cuban bartender, Roberto. The Cuban nodded and winked, then nudged Leandro who slowly turned around to greet Peter. Making no effort to mask his pleasure, Leandro freed a smile that engulfed his face—Eros erased inscrutability. Peter released his body; the Cuban was clearly no cause for alarm. Peter had known Roberto for several years as a partner in the ocean, not in sex. Frequently, they found themselves swimming in almost unconscious unison for half an hour or more. On land, even in the bar, they never more than nodded to each other. Now all three of them were laughing. Mockingly the Cuban suggested a swim, but Peter had already started for the door, with Leandro at his side.

Barely inside Peter's house, Leandro was suddenly seized by ferocity. Before the ripped-off clothing had firmly settled on the floor, Leandro had already pushed his cock into Peter's ass and started pinching his nipples into exquisite pain; furiously, he whipped Peter's cock into orgasm while collapsing into the pulsation of his own. Amazed and dazed, Peter stumbled into the kitchen to make a drink and to reorganize his senses. He returned to find Leandro crouched forward on his knees, slowly rolling his round ass and coyly smiling out at Peter from under an armpit. Peter was as startled by Leandro's sudden change in persona as he was by his own erection—he certainly did not want to remember how long it had been since his cock had proven capable of such a quick comeback. With slow deliberation, he took the proffered libation.

Peter was dozing into the dawn when Leandro abruptly shook him and demanded to leave immediately. He directed Peter to the entrance of a nearby beach, got out of the car and summarily announced his appearance at Peter's house for dinner the next night. He met Peter's desire to know where he lived with comic disdain and the explanation that he was cursed by his name to forever swim to and from whomever he loved. This time Leandro's laughter cracked slightly on an edge of anxiety. It was instantly clear to Peter that he would have to repress his voracious curiosity if he wished to continue—a stiff price but not as stiff as losing Leandro.

And so Leandro appeared almost daily, sometimes at

Peter's house, sometimes at Peter's beach, sometimes at the Attic, but always, he arrived by foot and had to be driven back to the entrance of the same beach. Peter's apprehension dissolved in growing trust. He was writing again. If he could write and have a relationship and be near the ocean, he was as whole as he could be.

Leandro spoke of his country but never by name. He spoke of riding horses and working the land; he indulged in no pride of ownership but was surely not a peasant. Once he flew into a rage when Peter half-jokingly mentioned the possibility of writing about El Salvador. He delivered a tiresome tirade about United States insensitivity to real Latin American needs and goals. He railed at Peter's complete lack of a coherent political ideology. He huffed on about the hopelessness of Peter's hermeticism, but gradually admitted to his own occasional indulgence in the useless luxuries of literature. He was fully conversant with Stendhal and Balzac, but García Lorca was the one he truly loved, with his words so rooted in blood and soil. Leandro knew long passages from the *Yerma* by heart. Swelling with passion, he would pour a torrent of Spanish into Peter's thirsty ears and then challenge him to provide a reciprocal experience in English. Peter quelled Leandro's skepticism with Faulkner. No matter whether the words were theirs, politic's, or literature's, they always ended in the mutual pleasure they took from each other's tongues.

A month of increasing fervor had almost fully replenished Peter's desiccated psyche, when Leandro abruptly informed him of his immediate departure—with such stern resoluteness that Peter hardened into stone silence. Would this be the last time he would see Leandro at the beach? He had for so long so totally acquiesced to Leandro's secretiveness that all his desperate questions were now hopelessly tangled around the swelling lump in his throat. He stopped the car. Leandro lunged across the

37

front seat almost crushing Peter with his embrace. He promised he would see Peter again, in one month, at most two. He leaped out of the car and yelled to Peter to drive away quickly, his words were ruptured by a sob. Peter drove home. He had to.

One month went by and Peter did, indeed, see Leandro again, but not as Leandro and not in the flesh. His name was someone else's, but the face and the hands were utterly unmistakable. He was in military fatigues accompanied by three other men, all with one arm raised in a clenched fist; their defiant smiles were dissolving in the graininess of the newsprint. All four were members of the Democratic Revolutionary Front. They had been assassinated. They had gotten no further than the front page of the *New York Times*.

Peter looked at the name again. The last name was the same as Manolo's.

Epilogue

Ariel had known the real name. What about Ariel? She who had known Leandro's real name, had she known the real man? Did she know how effortlessly he had moved from her bed to Peter's and back again? Was it fear or jealousy that prevented Peter from asking Ariel to share her knowledge, or was it a genuine kindness dictated by the residual warmth of their former relationship? Had Leandro fulfilled Ariel's dream as fully as he had Peter's? A dream that was now impossible to share, a dream that could only drive them further apart. How certain was his certainty that Ariel could not help him understand the full meaning of that sob Leandro released at his and Peter's final parting. That sob released on Ariel's stage, for the beach he had so regularly and obediently delivered Leandro to was the beach whose high dunes shielded Ariel's sprawling, shingled manse from the public. Had Leandro merely been some mocking guerrilla-gigolo? Could one have a relationship with someone who withheld his real name?

Whatever reality their fleeting partnership might have harbored lay mutely buried in that sob. Over and over again, Peter pleaded with his memory to release that sob to give it some form that would allay his worst fears. But like his own sadness, the sob grew ever more diffuse in its contour. Would he be forced to wait until the photograph in the *New York Times* had no more effect on him than on any casually unconcerned reader, before Leandro's image could be fulfilled?

No solution. No resolution. He considered curing his amorous hangover with yet another round of inebriation but simply lacked the energy. He indulged himself, instead, in utter inconsequence. Inconsequence was all he could handle. He sat at his writing/dining table, neither writing, nor dining, but dreamily drifting in and out of the ample plane of the window; he shaded the plane with his dark musings stopping just short of permitting it to reflect his true pain. He knew he could rely on the regularity and frequency of birds to arrest the coagulating layers of darkness and reassert the pane's transparency. A newly acquired birdbath had now been in place long enough to claim its role in the daily patterns of an ever-increasing variety of sight and song. An intrepid catbird had been the first to inaugurate the bath; with his vigorous preening and shaking, he seemed more intent on generating spray and spume than on actually bathing. Before resuming his rounds, the catbird locked eyes with Peter and froze in a pose that mirrored Peter's daze. Perhaps this species was as adept at human mimicry as at birdsong mime. The catbird reappeared on all but stormy days punctually at 10:10 A.M. Peter made sure to be seated by 10:00. Like some soap opera stoned housewife, he tuned the performance in. The catbird was always the opening; other birds were less bold and/or less punctual in their daily toilet. Golden finches arrived in chattering groups, but seldom would more than one take a furtive plunge. Perhaps too apprehensive of Peter's presence, they merely teased the tensile strength of the yellow cornflower stalks and rosebush branches surrounding the bath, before carrying their gossip elsewhere. Blue jays knew no such shyness; one or more would land like a well-aimed missile on the rim of the bath. Their strutting arrogance and coarse screeching overpowered the modest scale of the bowl; in a fury of wing-flapping, they vandalized the water. In spite of their stridency, he couldn't help admiring the handsomeness of their metallic blues and proudly peaking crests. More demure were the birds of brown that predominated in his temperate zone: the robin, the sparrow, the thrush, the nuthatch, the towhee (named by the shriek of his song), and the mourning dove so softly muted in color, shape, and sound. Rare was the appearance of the blazing yellow-chested oriole, more likely Peter would only hear his high-pitched rolling trill. Rarer still was the alarming beauty of the male cardinal's redness. A red so real and yet so evasive, not a primary red but somewhere blue. A red more suited to the tropics, one that might make a parrot proud. Peter held this idiosyncratic chroma responsible for the cardinal's shyness and scarceness. It was, of course, a cardinal that he always anticipated the most and almost never saw.

Rarest of all, and even more hoped for than a cardinal, was the diaphanous iridescence of the hummingbird. Ever since childhood, the aerodynamic impossibility of this minuscule creature had beguiled him. Amongst the hundreds of numbers Peter had found it necessary or convenient to memorize and store, twelve sixty was one of the very few to have persevered through the changing seasons, obsessions, addresses, locker combinations, telephones, sexual orientations, and computer access codes. One thousand two hundred and sixty was the number of heartbeats required to sustain the hummingbird's flickering translucence for one minute. How many wing beats per minute the heart generated he had more difficulty remembering, but he knew it was somewhere near four thousand in normal flight and some twelve thousand during the pyrotechnical diving displays performed by the male during courtship and/or aggression. Hyperkinetically stationary, visibly invisible, transparently mysterious, this bird becomes a jeweled metaphor of its function. The numbers are more eloquent than any adjectives seeking to catch its wonder. Would that he could direct his heartbeat so purposefully and efficiently.

It was to the hummingbird that he dedicated his garden, a task made easier by the fact that both he and hummingbirds needed red to survive. Hummingbirds and bees competed for the same nectar, but hummingbirds more exclusively claimed flowers of red, which quite often are long and tubular and point downward, making them more accessible to the hummingbird's long beak than to the bee. Then, too, red was not a color a bee could clearly see. And so he made a list of hummingbird flowers that stretched into early fall: foxglove, delphinium, trumpet vine, fuschia, dahlia, yucca, bee balm (one of many shared with the bee), salvia, cardinal flower (more imposing in its Latin, *Lobelia cardinalis*), butterfly bush, and others whose names he had lost. Many, but not all, were red. He wished his soil into the sumptuous and obsessive luxuriance of a Persian carpet, something like the soft, silken Saruk he had lost himself in as a child in his parental living room. Intertwined diamonds and hexagons dense with lush reds and purples, surrounded with borders of green and blue, with male cardinals and orioles in garlands of gold.

His imagination proved more fertile than his sandy soil. He ended with far more scruffiness than the juicy profusion he desired. He knew, of course, that there was but one species of hummingbird (the ruby-throated) partial to his clime and, like all hummingbirds, each member of the species was more than prone to be alone. Nonetheless, he spent many an hour awaiting this messenger that was far lighter than a letter. Hours largely spent in vain, even with the added inducement of a downward pointing beaker of sugared water with a red nipple (an appliance ugly enough to compromise the firmest fantasy). As much consolation as he could find came from the butterfly bushes, whose spindly branches were pulled into lazy arcs by the growing abundance of purple and magenta florets that counted out late July and August. They attracted flocks of regent and monarch butterflies, their velvet wings looping into airborne caresses of silence.

He weighted the weightlessness of the butterflies by making them the surrogates for his more customary summer companions, namely the bartenders, houseboys, waiters, and real estate agents who were usually the sole hope for erotic respite in an area dominated by couples. These now left him utterly indifferent. The ex-models anxiously guarding the remains of their artificial bodies and the discarded, fading boys who found their chances for minor successes easier in a resort than in a city, could only magnify the shattered pieces of his own, possibly illusory relationship. The previous summer he had taken perverse pleasure in sleeping with not one but three ex-boyfriends of a famous composer responsible for a significant increase in the local gay population; then sleeping with the composer himself. Now that memory made him squirm, as did his maudlin memories of this summer's tricks who had preceded Leandro, maybe even included Leandro. With no trace of embarrassment, he noted that his weary reveries had now surpassed in duration the actual time he had spent with Leandro. It had already been several weeks since the crickets and the katydids had started the first chorus of summer's final song. No matter. Let great men be great; he was a weary man being weary.

While his sexual inertia had an inner motivation, it also had an evermore alarming public complement. When friends had called him at the beginning of the summer to tell him of the growing rumors of gay cancer, he had dismissed their threatened tumors as some rabid right-wing hope. But then, words as yet new to him moved inexorably from the back to the front of the newspapers; and finally there were actual pictures of the poisonous purple bloom. Kaposi's sarcoma this viral hybrid was called, and soon the acronym for Acquired Immune Deficiency Syndrome became a familiar inhabitant of almost everyone's vocabulary. What had started in heterosexual asses in Africa seemed to have migrated, through official incompetence and private dalliance, and turned into a virulent homosexual plague. Conservative Christians vengefully pointed out their God's wrath; Republican columnists wondered at the advisability of homosexual waiters; straight friends balked at sharing drinks. Lines were being drawn. One of his best friends quickly unbested himself by suggesting Peter write a guidebook for straights about gay practices—what exotic things exactly went on in those water-front bars. Peter himself was as yet without apprehension, for no other reason than that Leandro had by now acquired such perfection that there was no possibility he might have carried such a vile infection.

Another war was beginning. Still he found himself unable to release the flow of ink across the lines of his paper pads. Notes, a dictionary, reading glasses, his pen, and paper were arranged every morning around the svelte swell and taper of his Chinese vase; but this ritual still life remained still and functioned only as the pedestal for the dance of his daydreams around the birdbath. Even an expensive new pen lacked the power to catalyze.

Slowly, as his garden began to crumble into fall's rusty palette, his focus shifted more and more to the ocean. Here he could not control or cultivate; here he had to give in to a vaster music. Here he risked total beauty. Here his loudest screams were only a whisper. The ocean absorbed all and released only what it desired to release. The constantly shifting rumble of its percussive patterns aroused but eluded comprehension. Peter's body, as always, found release in this rhyming vastness; direct access to the ocean was one of the very few possibilities he envied the rich for. He couldn't begin to tally up the hours he had spent drifting into the rippling reflections slowly gathering and rising into a swell that delivered the sun in a roll of foam at his feet, or else reaching out to the flaming glistening of the surface at sunset; or losing himself in the pearly thickness that slithered through an enveloping mist. Rollicking playfulness, magisterial calm, and roaring volumes of rage all engaged him equally. How often had the repetitive rhythms—always the same but always different—lured him into slumber on the beach? How often had that memory enchanted his nocturnal sleep? How often had he dreamed of merging the flow of his fluid body with that of the ocean? Free to swim, he swam to be free. Twice nearly drowning had not diminished his pleasure in the embrace of the Atlantic's effervescence, only made him more respectful. The drumming of the ocean had so often in the past encouraged the next character, the next line, or maybe just the next word to coalesce on the page when he returned home. Long-lost voices and images, sometimes welcome sometimes not, rode in the aftersplash of the waves' crash. That fall Leandro's name was so often washed in and out upon the waves that its shape was totally smoothed into amorphousness and finally and finely ground down to a grainy residue that was tenuously traced and erased on the shifting sand of the shore. The letters of the name surrendered their identity to abstract spirals and swirls.

It would only be a matter of measurable time, now,

before Peter would take up his pen and bury Leandro's sigh by
the sea.

Footnotes

For the Libretto of an As Yet Untitled Opera Commissioned for the 2000 Olympics at which the Music Competition Is to Be Reinstated

I

1)   Pindar, 12th Pythian Ode XII (ca. 490 B.C.). The specific flute Athena is credited with inventing, here is called the Phrygian flute; it is a double flute thought to have been formed by her out of stag's bones or horns.

2)   C. W. Frampton, *The Origins of Modern Woodwind Instruments*, University of New Mexico, Albuquerque, 1963, p. 27. This proposal seems more speculative than Frampton's earlier one that suggested the blowing or sucking out of marrow generated the flutes without side holes found in Paleolithic excavations.

3)   The sexual innuendo implicit in Aphrodite's mockery of Athena's Phrygian flute is reinforced in Plato's Minos, where Athena refers to the two appendages of the flute as "shameful things, an outrage to my body. I yield me not to such baseness."

4)   These Platonic rejections of the flute were later taken up by Aristotle in his *Politics VIII*, where the instrument is reviled as having "nothing to do with the mind."

5)   Pindar, Pythian Ode XII, for Midas of Aphragas, winner in flute playing.

6)   This conjunction of "tail" and "spin" did not come

into English usage until around 1910 and is clearly part of Rouse's attempt to emulate Homer's vernacular tone, rather than render a literal translation.

7)   Frampton, op cit, p. 6. This fragment of a satyr play generally attributed to the third-century B.C. writer Nossis ends, "Marsyas subdued the violence of his breath and drew Zephry's rage into grace." While many Greek writers claimed Marsyas's flute continued to play by itself those tunes Athena had blown into it before she hurled it to earth, Nossis, like Euripides, was more willing to credit Marsyas with actually founding the rules of the flute.

8)   Philip Bate, *The Flute*, W. W. Norton & Co., New York, 1957, p. 57.

9)   Hyginus has confused the musical contest between Apollo and Marsyas with that of Apollo and Pan. It is unclear from the extant texts whether Pliny himself was confused or whether he simply chose to make his character confused.

10)   Since 1991, replaced by the term "hubris pill."

11)   The first Olympiad took place in 776 B.C. and was held regularly every four years until A.D. 393. In addition, there were the Pythian, Nemean, and Isthmian contests.

12)   By the fifth century B.C., flute playing was the only musical competition still taking place at the Games. Chariot racing, wrestling, horse racing, and boxing were among the other eleven contests.

13)   This lost sculpture by Zeuxis is the earliest known representation of Marsyas. Possibly the myth of Apollo and Marsyas did not fully evolve until the fifth century B.C. From then on, Apollo and Marsyas figure on the vases of the Kleophon Painter and a succession of anonymous artists.

14)   Song more than purely instrumental music would naturally be favored by Greek writers.

15)   Roman Jakobson, *Language in Literature*, Harvard

University Press, Cambridge, Mass., 1987, p. 463. Historically it would be more accurate to say that the movie camera's lens sees Homerically.

16)   Such ithyphallic characters were not found again in Europe until the sixteenth century.

17)   Ernest Hemingway, in *A Farewell to Arms*, condenses this tale even further by simply having a woman of Abruzzi say, "It was bad for the girls to hear the flute at night."

18)   George Bataille, *The Tears of Eros*, City Lights Books, San Francisco, Calif., 1989, pp. 73–74.

19)   From the Greek word "athlos" meaning "contest." The first use of the word seems to be in Homer's *Odyssey* (Book XVIII), when Euryalus mocks Ulysses' weary refusal to take part in the games at Alcinous's palace: "I see not of a man expert in feats athletic."

20)   The primacy wrestling held in Greek culture can be gauged, as well, from Homer's many references to it. In the twenty-third book of the *Iliad*, it is the wrestling match that promises the biggest prize, at the games held at the funeral rites of Patroclus. The loser receives "a woman well skilled in women's work, valued at four oxen," which is the same prize the winner of the chariot race receives.

21)   Plato also refers to a "winged chariot," in *The Phaedrus*.

22)   In Icaromenippus (ca. 160 A.D.), Lucian equipped Menippus with one wing from an eagle and another from a vulture to fly to Mount Olympus. He was propelled to the moon on a giant waterspout.

23)   Zeus's prayer holes bear uncanny resemblance to late twentieth century images of Moon craters.

24)   Plato's Atlantis is linked, by modern archaelogists, to the recently excavated island of Thera, which is a remnant of a

much larger island destroyed by a volcanic eruption around 1500 B.C.

25)   Where Thetis held him when she dipped him into the River Styx in order to ensure his physical invulnerability.

26)   Venus drawing an anemone from the dying Adonis's blood and Apollo's tears mixing with Hyacinthus's blood to form a hyacinth are perhaps the most well-known examples of this phenomenon.

II

1)   This is the second time Lucian makes Mercury the vehicle for Menippus's reentry.

2)   John F. Gilbey, *Western Boxing and World Wrestling*, North Atlantic Books, Berkeley, Calif., 1986, p. 83. Gilbey never identifies the "expert" referred to here and elsewhere, but denies his contention that both dancing and procreation were derived from wrestling.

3)   Many of these holds can be seen on the tomb reliefs at Beni Hassan (2380–2167 B.C.) on the Nile.

4)   Gilbey, op cit., p. 90. The law of Ulpian.

5)   Wrestling first became part of the Olympiad in 704 B.C.

6)   Given wrestling's growing importance in Greek culture, it is not as remarkable as these modern commentators have suggested, to find Socrates and the young Alcibiades wrestling at a palestra in Plato's *Symposium*. Echoing Plato, Aristotle found wrestling "salubrious for the mind."

7)   Milon of Croton was as renowned for this hold as he was for his ability to carry an ox around the stadium and killing it with one punch.

8)   Pindar, Nemean VI, for Alkimidas of Aegina, winner in the boys' wrestling (ca. 461 B.C.).

9)   In Pythian VIII, Pindar continues these musical ana-logies: "To let your eyes rain melody/ on every step that I take."

10)   Seen on many Red Figure vessels and still employed in wrestling today, the hold immediately preceded Heracles's fatal chokehold on the Nemean lion.

11)   This is the only wrestling event that is a seminal part of Judeo-Christian mythology.

12)   Gilbey, op cit., p. 91. Gilbey's contention that "Israel" is thought to mean a "wrestler with God" runs counter to the accepted Hebrew meaning of "Israel" ("God perserveres").

13)   Beyond this, Athena and Jesus, of course, were both parthenogenetic.

14)   A chariot of similar design, composed of three-headed vultures, is observed by Menippus on the moon.

15)   Plutarch also pictures the moon (*The Face of the Moon*, ca. 1000 A.D.) as a kind of second earth populated with demons living in caves.

16)   George Steiner, *After Babel*, Oxford University Press, London, 1975, p. 401.

17)   This version of the Pan pipe is made from an alder-shoot from which the bark has been stripped.

18)   The tears of Marsyas condensed into a spring that then became the source of the clearest river in Phrygia.

III

1)   In Consulting the Oracle of Hades, Lucian has Men-ippus return to the surface of the earth via a crossing through a hidden interior artery.

2)   This disguise was ambiguous enough so that Men-ippus could alternately be taken for Ulysses, Hercules, or Orpheus.

3)   Not only for Columbus, but for many other fifteenth-

century navigators, especially the Portuguese, the primary motives were to reach Cathay or to discover Atlantis.

4)   The other method of reaching the Moon discussed by Cyrano and De Guiche is still more fabulous and entails an iron chariot drawn upward by magnets that are continually thrown ahead of it by the driver.

5)   Stanley Goldstein, *Reaching for the Stars*, Praeger, New York, 1987, p. 46.

6)   Harley Earle was the designer who introduced the tail fin to the Cadillac in 1948, and he was largely responsible for the "aircraft styling" so typical of American automobiles of this era.

7)   Peter K. Vogel, *The American Dream Machine*, D. H. Ingersoll Press, Los Angeles, Calif., 1977, p. 154.

8)   Michael R. Ball, *Professional Wrestling as Ritual Drama in American Popular Culture*, Edwin Mellen Press, Lewiston, New York, 1983, p. 21.

9)   Ibid., p. 6. Although Ball refers to wrestling as the "great American Passion play," his basic thesis is Marxist driven and emphasizes the notion of modern wrestling as a ritual of elitist social manipulation and control.

10)   Roland Barthes, *Mythologies*, The Noonday Press, New York, 1992 ed., p. 21. While Barthes, like Ball, sees wrestling as a ritual spectacle rather than a sport, he sees it in a positive light that illuminates "the ancient myth of public Suffering and Humiliation: the cross and the pillory."

11)   The first of three Stations where Christ falls down.

12)   Even more consequent to wrestling's resurgence in the late 1940s was the advent of television.

13)   Sufficient visual and technical similarities do not exist to support Franklin's comparison of Sputnik with the V-2 rocket. He himself seems to be a victim of the aggression underlying

the rampant enthusiasm and anxiety of the space race that he seeks to analyze.

14)   It does seem ironic that the Cadillac tail fins had been completely removed by 1965, during the very height of America's rocket obsessiveness. But, in point of fact, the actual laws of aerodynamics, rather than the look of Earle's "aircraft styling" now began to rule automotive design.

15)   Goldstein, op cit., p. 5.

16)   E.g., "I kindle light with flaming songs" (Pindar, Olympian IX, for Epharomostos of Opous, winner in the wrestling).

17)   Repeatedly referred to by Xenophon as "celestial mechanics."

18)   These attempts at weather control pioneered by Von Neuman preoccupied almost as many physicists, in the 1950s and 1960s, as did space exploration.

19)   James Gleick, *Chaos*, Viking Penguin, New York, 1987, p. 313. It remains moot whether this newer model of liquid crystallization might make weather control possible.

IV

1)   Although the most often quoted of the dedicatory speeches, this was but one of many that transformed the Brooklyn Bridge into a passageway into utopia.

2)   Hapnell took this hyperbole quite literally and sought to set up an international committee to proclaim the bridge the Eighth Wonder of the World.

3)   Alan Trachtenberg, *Brooklyn Bridge, Fact and Symbol*, University of Chicago Press, 1965, p. 68.

4)   Roebling's belief in the sovereignty of reason did not preclude him from becoming involved with this kind of millen-

nial mysticism, and the teachings of the so-called "Poughkeepsie Seer" were quite important to him.

5)   This surely is a confusion of "adrogyne" with "hermaphrodite."

6)   The secret son of Poseidon and the cousin of Heracles, Theseus, together with Heracles and Hermes, was a patron of all the palestras. His wrestling contest with the ogre Sinis led many to credit him with founding modern wrestling.

7)   Not to be confused with the cross-buttock move.

8)   Until the fifth century B.C., Greek wrestlers performed nude.

9)   Fittingly the publication date (1865) of *From the Earth to the Moon* is the same year as Roebling's founding of the company that was to build the Brooklyn Bridge.

10)   Verne's calculations for the velocity necessary to overcome gravity (25,000 mph) were accurate. The launch in Florida was preceded by an animal test flight.

11)   The cat ate the squirrel.

12)   This theme is reiterated in Verse IV (Cape Hatteras), where the Wright Brothers become "windwrestlers" who "ride / The blue's cloud-templed districts unto ether . . ."

13)   Crane moved to New York City in 1923 in order to live in sight of the bridge he would mythologize in his final work.

14)   Although Walt Whitman is more frequently named than the author of the *Iliad*, the self-consciously Olympian tone of *The Bridge* and its classicizing similes constantly invoke Homer.

15)   At this Station, Christ met his mother.

16)   Betty Mary Spears, *History of Sport and Physical Activity in the United States*, Wm. C. Brown & Co., Dubuque, Iowa, 1978, p. 37.

17)   Crane had already introduced these musical and

nautical metaphors in the introductory verse (e.g., "harp and altar," "choiring strings," "... and of the curveship lend a myth to God").

18)   The only athlete celebrated by Pindar who competed in both wrestling and chariot racing, at the Nemean Games.

19)   In this final stanza, Cathay and Atlantis are conflated as the "upward veering bridge seeks its final destination."

20)   Steiner, op cit., p. 401.

21)   "Stars scribble on our eyes the frosty sagas / The gleaming cantos of unvanquished space" (Verse IV, Cape Hatteras).

V

1)   The catenary curve is formed by a rope or cable hanging freely between two fixed points and supports the greatest possible weight with the least tension at the point of suspension.

2)   He was the only poet drawn to orchestrate the cables of this bridge.

3)   E. Norman Gardner, "Wrestling," *Journal of Hellenic Studies*, London, 1905, vol. 25, p. 17.

4)   Athena is generally credited with instructing Theseus in the art of wrestling, but Hermes is its Olympian inventor. The Greek wrestling gymnasiums bore his daughter Palestra's name.

5)   Gardner, op cit., p. 20. This analysis of the contest between Ulysses and Ajax (*Iliad*, Book XXIII), together with the subsequent analyses of Attic vase depictions comprise the most thorough study of the relationship of the holds of England's Cumberland Westmoreland wrestling to Greek wrestling.

6)   M. Briggs Hunt, *Greco-Roman Wrestling*, Ronald Press Co., New York, 1964, p. 72.

7) Jake Pfeffer was the 1930s wrestling impresario who invented this blood capsule and prided himself on the freakishness of his wrestlers ("You can't get a dollar with a normal looking guy.").

8) The tag teams "Demolition" and "Ax and Smash" embody some of these more recent stereotypes.

9) Although Barbanelli's scholarly rigors have failed, thus far, to identify the Christian fathers who initiated the almost universal removal from or mutilation of male genitalia on classical statuary, this monograph on the Barberini Faun remains seminal.

10) Very little is known about Amico di Sandro or what his inspiration was for this unconventional and unique depiction of the adult Christ with a visible male organ.

11) Satyrs, of course, were the models for these medieval representations of devils.

12) Closer to the blue of the sky in Giovanni Bellini's "Saint Francis," this blue is very different from the "Robin's Egg Blue" so prevalent on the El Dorados of the 1950s.

13) Even Pravda employed these analogies and referred to Gagarin's space capsule Vostok as an "ariel chariot" (April 13, 1961, p. 1).

14) The word "horsepower" was simply incorporated into the vocabulary of these aeronautic obsessions.

15) On this same day (July 16), twenty-four years earlier the first atom bomb was detonated.

16) Burroughs concurs with Crowley that "the human body is much too dense for space conditions" and, on page 3 of the above-mentioned text, concludes, "The shift from time to space may involve mutations as drastic and irreversible as the shift from water to land."

17) Diana would obviously have been a more appropriate choice, since she is the goddess of the moon; and her brother

Apollo is the god of the sun. But NASA officials were loathe to choose a female patron for their missions.

18)   This ceremony is not unlike the Mayan ritual in which blood from the pierced foreskin is collected on a piece of paper and thrown into a fire to produce visions of the gods.

19)   Gleick, op cit., p. 314. These states of crystallization are referred to as "nonequilibrium phenomena . . . They are the products of imbalance from one piece of nature to another."

VI

1)   Thrasymedes' tunnel from Hades is clearly indebted to the one found in Lucian's Menippian voyage, but the labial folds that camouflage the entrance and his protagonist's "brazen spear" adumbrate this tale with a more erotic charge.

2)   P. Levi, *History of Greek Literature*, Viking, London, 1985, p. 33.

3)   "Nevertheless awake the fine strings of the harp / And turn your thoughts to wrestling" (Pindar, Nemean X, for Theioas of Argos, a wrestler).

4)   Now known as the "near side cradle" hold.

5)   The Greeks referred to this hold as "flying mare."

6)   "Acheiropoietos" is the Greek word for these so-called "paranormal" images.

7)   Eva Kuryluk, *Veronica and Her Cloth*, Basil Blackwell Inc., Cambridge, Mass., 1991, p. 5.

8)   Ibid., p. 52. This correlation of the transference of Christ's bleeding and sweating face to Veronica's cloth with female menstruation is the primary premise of Kuryluk's book.

9)   In Judaism, the blood shed at circumcision is also considered as sacred ink.

10)   Most of the scientists with STURP (The Shroud of

Turin Research Project) had previously been involved with the nuclear space probe and military technology.

11)   Only the invention of photography had been able to make the image on the Shroud of Turin clearly visible. The Shroud itself is a negative image that becomes positive when seen in photographic negative.

12)   Frank C. Tribble, *Portrait of Jesus?* Stein and Day, New York, 1983, p. 36: " . . . microchemical tests detected no pigment binders, or other foreign substances to a level of less than one-millionth of a gram, thus totally demolishing any claim that paint had been used . . ."

13)   Ibid., p. 253. The contention that light radiation not heat radiation is responsible for the image might also be proposed for the transference of the image of the Gorgon Medusa's head to the reflective shield loaned to Perseus by Athena.

14)   This episode is most vividly recounted in Ovid's *Metamorphosis*, 4.

15)   Known as "release."

16)   In Book XVIII of the *Iliad*, Homer's elaborate description of the microcosm depicted on Achilles' new armor seems to all but overlook his physical invulnerability (but for his heel). Indeed, Achilles would have no need for armor.

17)   The "guillotine" hold seems more an invention of modern wrestling.

18)   While Marsyas's skin was hung on a tree, in the Aztec ritual of Tlacaxiphehualiztli, the priests actually donned the flayed skins of the sacrificial victims, in emulation of the golden cloak of Xipe Totec, in order to ensure the success of the new harvest.

19)   Also known as "Our Lord the Flayed One" and "Yopi."

20)   There is no known Aztec or Mayan glyph for "statue."

21)   Burroughs continues (p. 82), "However, we have a model to hand that is much less dense in fact almost weightless: the astral or dream body." Neither he nor Crowley have yet to explore how these transformations might relate to Gleick's "Chaotic Harmonies."

South Brooklyn Casket Company

He was sitting in the steam room of the gym; he had one left finger up the ass of the guy next to him. No, two fingers. But he was thinking of the expressway.

"Normal traffic conditions ahead," the mechanical story board blinked out overhead. He kept trying to remember the last name of the art critic whose car hit a tree, killing him and his passenger mother. Many suspicions were left behind. Gene was his first name.

"Oh Man, let me sit on your dick." He wondered why the steam room was so undisturbed today. Usually, at this hour, there were three old men discussing the good old days when all you needed was a horse to carry the plot of a movie through. He had come here hoping the physical steam might release some of his mental steam. His fingers momentarily explored, more aggressively, the membrane of the asshole. Was all the anger in his left hand?

"DELAY EXITS 59–57" rolled across the story board. His mother had inhaled almost the entire space of the car as soon as she had gotten in. If his house had withstood implosion for eight days, surely his car could withstand this two-hour trial. She began punctuating his suffocation with yet another rambling verse of her lullaby of hostility. Couldn't your boyfriend help you more; your sister-in-law never would have gotten your brother if I hadn't told him it was time to leave my house; I don't understand why that ugly blue chair is in the middle of all your beautiful furniture; you certainly spoiled me with your cooking, do the two of you eat like that when you are alone; you're too generous, he's too lazy, she's too greedy, your sister's ugly teeth will ruin her career. Did you love your father?

In his earliest days in Paris, Pablo Picasso admired a gritty illustrator of the disenfranchised who was named George Bottini. George Bottini suffered from tertiary syphilis and began to break down mentally as well as physically. One night, after dinner, he tried to kill his mother with a large kitchen knife. He died several months later in a straitjacket. Syphilis was very common at the turn of the century.

At Exit 58, "delays" arrived as one long, slow singular; and she went into the reprieve of her decrepitude. Every day gets worse, nothing to look forward to, no more high heels, a bank is managing my stocks now, only my children keep me alive, I can't remember when my memory lapse started, where should my ashes go if I'm cremated, I better do my will soon. As if her will were the only will she had left. But no one can see she had a stroke, and her new boyfriend is twelve years younger than she is.

He knew this body; his fingers were no strangers to its ass, his cock no stranger to its mouth. Several times he had interluded with it like this before. A body the same age as his, but more artificially sculpted by weight-lifting—although not to the point of being countersensuous. When clothed, the body was very butch clone (tight jeans, black boots, cropped mustache, etc.); naked, it was another story.

At Exit 50, she began to love his dog; how sweet he had become, how much he seemed to like her now. Only she called him by the name of his first dog. His first dog had been the only confidant of his troubled youth. His mother had had the dog put to sleep after he left for prep school. He had never forgiven her. Was this name scramble a simple memory lapse? Was he exaggerating the subtext?

He began to think of horseshoe crabs, coupling at the bay in the late spring—grinding in the sand with all the weighty slow motion of their prehistory. Then he remembered someone telling him that as you get older, you produce more earwax. He wondered if there was a correlation between more earwax and less semen. The steam went on again; and he noticed, for the first time, that he had a hard-on.

Once more, NORMAL TRAFFIC CONDITIONS AHEAD blinked on overhead. He and she had a confrontation. It was the one about mates—his and his brother's. It remained inconceivable to her that either he or his brother might indeed be fortunate to have the partner he had. Did he ever miss going out with females? Thank God he hadn't chosen George (a friend whose too obvious homosexuality gave her the shakes). At least, there was no alcohol in the car. His mother's acceptance of his sexuality grew more reluctant with each cocktail she consumed.

The door opened. Very quickly, he withdrew his fingers and crossed his legs to hide his erection. Smooth-skinned, well-toned, the new entrant was obviously cruising, but showed little interest in the two older bodies. Still, this younger one lingered. He, in turn, began to trouble himself with some of his own recent memory lapses. While shopping for dinner, he lost the name "Romaine." Twice, recently, he had blanked out on who his next-door neighbor was. And, when he really needed it, "reverberation" evaporated for two hours.

At Exit 42, he knew it wouldn't be much longer. She was dozing. He was confused. Where was the space for his drama? How real was his adult memory of his victory over his childhood victimization? How real his mother's contradictory screenplay of the love and gilded ease of his youth? A shadow began to enshroud her slumber, making her very vulnerable. Involuntarily, he began to smile at his brother's insistence that all Jewish women cut watermelon with a huge knife, and then remove every last seed before bringing the melon to the table.

There couldn't be much time left before another interruption. He began to concentrate on the ass. He knew just where to bend his fingers, how to massage that gland. He knew he was inducing that frantic tingling that extended into the cock and made it still more rigid and furious to come. Now the body was like a puppet on his hand, writhing and moaning at his fingers' command. His hand even seemed responsible for the spasms of sexpleading words. He wondered how long he could make this play go on.

They were at Exit 33, and he knew how it would end, now. At curbside, he would tip the baggage handler who would get a wheelchair and bring his mother to the ticket counter. She wasn't crippled, but she didn't like the long walk through the airport. Even though he knew this, he would feel pangs of guilt and sympathy while watching the back of the wheelchair being rolled into the distance. It compromised his anger.

"I said, 'Blow me,'" he said. And he watched the lips anxiously engorge the length of his cock as he heard the door opening.

Another Winter

Daily, the city became more difficult to imagine. Shadows were robbing metaphor of its necessary light. Abject poverty and abject wealth had appropriated all the hues of meaninglessness. What words were left left little hope for nourishment. Even thoughts of the bygone summer lacked real sustenance. Progress's greed had made his need for sunlight carcinogenic. Hospitals had spiked the rolling tides with hypodermic needles and viral waste. Inhabitants of the city were told the gaseous swelter they were gagging on was the combined result of the presence of ozone on the ground and the absence of ozone in the atmosphere. Industrial exhaust was exhausting life; science fiction was sliding out of the future tense. For many, the death penalty was the only answer. For others, more self-indulgence would have to do. He inclined to the latter; but it was no longer an easy matter. Not just seduction but even desire had acquired the aloof spell of artifacts from a distant culture—and middle age alone was not to blame.

As he slurped through the morbid slush of rain and snow, he battled with the apprehension of seeing yet again, one more face with "sex kills" written across gaunt flesh. He descended the steps of the subway to find the local homeless straightening out their sheets of newspaper on their soggy cardboard mattresses. This communal ritual of domesticity momentarily left only the silence of fermenting piss and sweat to assault anxious sensibilities. On the platform, a girl/woman made bulbously top-heavy and grotesquely ageless by Down's syndrome was convulsively laughing and pleading with two cops to make her their guard dog. She bit her hands and gleefully barked to prove her canine capabilities. "Have a nice day," they all said.

In the subway, he read and silently recited the familiar litanies of threat and abstention that had gradually displaced the advertisements glamorizing smoking and drinking. With the exception of an occasional exhortation to phone sex, the placards piously devoted space to Fraud/Abuse, drug addiction; Pregnant? We can help, and the pathetically punning plea not to go out without your rubbers. More strident were the pleas of the scarred and scabbed who lurched through, one per car per stop, rattling coin-filled cups and battered lives. "Have a nice day," they all said.

He got off at 23rd Street to go to the Y for one of his thrice-weekly battles with entropy. Mindless maintenance was demanding more and more of his time. The drudge of bodybuilding was partially relieved by the bracing sweat of steam bath and sauna, and the nakedness that sported an endless variety of cocks. Once upon a time, this had led to a belated return to adolescent sessions of mutual masturbation, or even to a hurried anonymous tryst. Now the voyeuristic act of classification had to suffice as an end in itself. In the shower, his customary relish in the lavish lather proffered by a brand-new bar of soap was interrupted by the simultaneous leer of three old men with nearly identical uncut cocks, their shriveled masculinity vainly struggling out from under cascading floods of abdominal folds. "Have a nice day," they all said.

The only solution was to leave. To leave behind the smelled but unseen sunsets. To leave behind the dank and horizonless mine shaft of the city to brood by itself over its exhausted veins. To lose himself in the endless stanzas of the sea. To see sun and horizon.

On the plane, just the thought of South smoothed his face with near beatitude. For a long time South had meant Quintana Roo—a name and a place that simply sparkled—a state and a state of mind that separated the silky undulation of the Caribbean from the weightier rhythms of the Yucatán. But in the fall, a hurricane's rage had blighted this delight; so South would now be farther south and be Costa Rica. Could a country named "rich in coasts" be wrong?

A night in Costa Rica's capital still separated him from the sea. What he noticed most in San Jose was the total absence of mucous guttural sputter that curdled the cold of North's winter. The food, unfortunately, was all politeness. The subtly orchestrated fierceness of earth and fire that ravished the tongue in Mexico was nowhere to be tasted there. But, in the morning, the hoped-for delirium began as he drove into the constantly shifting kaleidoscope of Costa Rica's landscapes. Atlantic and Pacific, cloud forest and rain forest, active volcano and fertile farmed valley, sun and rain, cold and hot raced and replaced each other in dream's speed. The narrowness of the country seemed only to have multiplied and intensified its diversity. His goal was southwest, but the mountains first forced the road southeast; San José was quickly superseded by a cloud forest. Pine-bearing rocks and spuming waterfalls appeared, disappeared, and reappeared in an endless unfurling of puffing whiteness. He floated over the ever-twisting road as though his car were being propelled by the brush of a Chinese wash drawing.

He quickly descended from clouds into clarity to glide through a green valley. Clumps of tall white and fleshy pink lilies, heavy with their narcotic stamens, slowly swung under the sun. He knew them from another dream. "Queen of the Night," their lush but harsh seduction was called. He stopped to pick a few. The air was hot but crystalline, radiant with the exhalation of a scent that evaporated on the threshold of his nostrils' knowledge. The valley opened into relentless flatness; and clouds once more enveloped his path—clouds of dirt rising from a rocky, unpaved road. As straight as it was bumpy, the road bounced by countless, stiff battalions of pine trees and banana palms. The Pacific Ocean, he knew, was on his right, and all was right.

Slowness and sameness blurred into uncounted hours until the straightness finally gave way to the town of Quepos and steep cliffs that paralleled the ocean's horizon. On one of these cliffs, a farm and a guest house were precipitously inclined over the ocean below. This radically tilted plane was to be his retreat. The caretaker showed him into one of four rooms that shared an interior courtyard and a vine-enshrouded veranda perched at mid-tree height with the Pacific in sight.

He rushed to wash away the city's residue in the warm and briny bubbling of the ocean. He was too exhausted to notice much except the water lapping at his flesh and the velvet feeling underfoot on the beach. The sand was softer, finer, far denser and grayer than the sand on North's shores. He was only peripherally aware of the long, lean, assless man who so purposefully brushed by him on this deserted strand. He was even less aware of the steamy chatter that enveloped him as he passed through the band of palm trees on his way back up the hill. Dinner served by the caretaker on the verandah was as bland as it was welcome. The thick thud of a sloth falling out of the vines above sent both the sloth and him packing. He willingly surrendered his consciousness to the waves' polyphonic prose.

He woke up in a wailing whirlpool of sound. A high-pitched, relentlessly circling shriek, like the mournful, morning supplication of some frenzied, monkish cult. Struggle as he might, he couldn't rise to the surface of this shrillness; willingly or not he slowly sank into the regularity of its revolutions. Soon the saturated pitch began to soothe. Abruptly, it stopped. He couldn't yet see, but he already knew this hyper-chant emanated from the hind legs of a virtuoso species of cricket that he had never encountered before. This was the sunrise raga that was daily to precipitate his awakening; and, just as regularly, it would lure the sun back into the ocean to the accompaniment of a fanfare of orange and flame.

Here, so often, sound not sight would initiate sense. His eyes, when he looked up, flinched and vibrated with vibrations counter to those of the pulsing light; when he looked down, his eyes rolled helplessly in a flood of waxy luxuriance. Only reluctantly would the lascivious turbulence surrender to the desire for categorization. For several days, orchid, lily, morning glory, and the cascading heliconia were only lurid flickerings on the racing torrents of green. Land crabs were flashes of lapis lazuli and hummingbirds an enameled disturbance of the air. Lovebirds could only be perceived as the staccato of some frantic sonata. He recognized the parrots' cackling screech, but could see no trace of its instrument's case.

Very slowly would sound acquire shape, and order tune the tropical cacophony. The screech turned acid green, and the chattering in the palm trees into a flurry of snowy white that masked the faces of a rollicking troupe of squirrel monkeys. The hummingbird surrendered its transparent suspension to gravity just long enough to acquire the weight of classification. All, of course, performed on a schedule whose logic was readily synchronized with that of his wrist-watch. The cricket chant at 5:30 A.M., the entrance of parrots at 7:15 A.M., followed by hummingbirds, red-winged blackbirds, and countless finches. At 8:00 A.M., pelicans glided by in a sail formation, anxious to fill the copious buckets of their beaks. By noon, all had built into a Technicolor crescendo that slowly reversed itself in the course of the afternoon—until the cricket chanted all into the husk of dusk.

His schedule unwound in spirals of more subjective needs. In the morning, he simply camouflaged himself in the fluctuations of flora and fauna. In the afternoon, he gave his body to the ocean—swimming long and slowly or just floating on the roll of the surface. When the waves permitted, he climbed onto the phantom spires of the pocked rock outcroppings that framed the ocean's shallows to watch the tide write its rhythms on the grainy softness of the sand, until he too would be called into dusk by the crickets' wail. Dinner, sleep, and cricket chant again.

As individual species of birds, crabs, flowers, shrubs, and trees began to grow and root in his awareness, so too did his own physicality. And so it transpired that one afternoon he was diverted from the puzzle of the zigzagging intaglio maze being made by tiny snails just below the surface of the sand to the more solvable puzzle of the path made by a variety of single males, a path that lost itself in a low wall of rocks. Amongst the makers of this trail, he recognized the thin, assless man who had brushed by him on the first day. This same man now smiled at him all too familiarly. He waited just long enough for the man to disappear behind the rocks, then followed. The wall hid from sight a tranquil cove where some fifteen men lay alone or with a partner. A resting herd basking in sun and arousal. In his haste to avoid the leer of the one he had followed, his eyes fell into those of a languid, burnished black-haired youth lying on his back, the only celebrant who had kept on his bathing suit. The scant suit's tightness was as brazen as the smile that slid from torrid welcome to cool disdain and back again. All this with just enough humor to forestall intimidation. The slightest flash of the youth's dark eyes and the nearly imperceptible nod of his head were quickly welcomed as an invitation to join him. He sat down. They appreciatively appraised each other. Words were not immediately needed. He became acutely aware of the efforts of all the other sunbathers to siphon off for themselves some of the energy of this newly possible liaison. Sufficiently encouraged, he was about to risk a declarative verbal or physical gesture, when the youth rolled over and turned his muscular back to him in order to light a cigarette. Glistening sand cascaded down the rippling backside. His fixed gaze, the reflective intensity of the sun, together with the sliding crystals of sand triggered a hallucinatory dance of purplish sunspots. As his hand reached out through his entrancement, the whirl of discs disappeared. No sooner did they disappear than they reappeared—but now in stationary randomness emblazoned on the youth's back. His hand recoiled with unknown speed. North seized his consciousness and banished all joy as his eyes riveted on the dire monogram of the plague his dreams had never dreamed of here.

"You shouldn't be in the sun. It's dangerous for you," He was speaking to the back.

The youth rolled over to face him once again. The meaning of his smile was now lost in an exasperation of opacity.

He pleaded with the smile, "Don't you speak English?"

The smile slowly ebbed into the lips' labors to shape the sounds of another's tongue. Flatly he intoned, "Virgil is still the Frog Boy."

Short End

1990

The letters looped lackadaisically, loosely tumbling into and out of configurations of words, sometimes legibly, sometimes not. Often meaning was completely erased by the autoerotic pleasure that the letters released in the wake of their wayward trails. There was more joy in his left hand than in his right; there was drawing in his left hand. There was also occasionally a violence he had never seen before. It was that time in August when summer became finite. He was trying to write with his left hand. It looked like drunken calligraphy.

The summer had been like that: wayward, fitful, often quite painful. He remembered spending an undue amount of time visiting a close friend in an emergency room, brooding on that institutional purgatory and what a bad name it gave to death. The friend was filled with so much love at the end that maybe that was what killed him. Others had died, too; but they weren't as close. He had spent so much time in the city this summer that the sound of the ocean and the sound of the subway merged into a rolling hiss of fuck shit piss fuck shit piss. And in the subways, where were the homeless and the rats? Was the stumpy, ponderous carcass that for so long refused to be washed away by the tide, that of a mutilated seal, as most claimed, or was it the bloated body of a homeless-eating rat?

His left-handed writing interrupted his homeless narrative with dreams of Peter. Out-of-control *es* and *ys* turned into a cascade of piss. Peter standing at the top of a narrow stairway and urinating in a giant arc down onto him. "I am the piss Christ baptizing you the censorious senator." And then outrageous laughter. Something like that but less topical was the way they had met, more or less. Him picking Peter up; and Peter sucking his reluctant sexuality fully into the open for the first time, then staggering drunkenly through darkness in search of a toilet only to piss all over his host's bookcase, claiming a territory he would not soon relinquish (perhaps, would not soon be permitted to relinquish). Peter not only had permitted him his sexuality, but permitted him to laugh. They laughed for four months before they settled down to the serious interchangeability of I and he, lived and written.

Warily, he walked down his building's stairs, arousing his defenses for the subway and the emergency room. Through the iron grate of the gate to the street, he saw a dazed sparrow flapping on the sidewalk, then a big black boot purposefully crushing it into a brittle crunch of grayness. Simultaneously, the sneering shaven head that belonged to the boot turned to him and spat out, "faggot." At least they weren't going in the same direction. In the summer, small favors were the most the city could offer.

Another voice. All summer he had been looking for another voice, and now August was calling to autumn and Peter was still able to gnaw at his present. There had been no Peter since Salvador, not in Berlin, not in Costa Rica, not elsewhere. Quite some time had actually passed since they had stopped inventing each other; but, although much of Peter had been banished from the realm of I into a more anonymous he-ness, he still clung tenaciously to some precipice of the imagination. Who was it that had taunted, "A painter can paint like the ocean but you can't write like the ocean"? I or he? Maybe the look meant more than the meaning, but, of course, no one would ever see his left-handedness. No one would see those vagrant *w*s flapping awkwardly like the whooshing wings of mourning doves. Maybe that was the point.

On the way to the subway he saw a butterfly maintaining a precarious grip on a hairdresser's window behind which a bromeliad bloomed. "Too poignant," he thought. He didn't recognize anyone in the emergency room.

Black Rainbow

Had he seen it, or was it merely a smear on the windows momentarily claiming form? Was it perhaps a hallucination induced by his frustration? Had he been its only witness?

Slowly, surprise and questioning receded, and his normal vision was restored. Shimmering grayness reestablished its rule outside and inside. The blur of the darkness began to slow the whirling in his head. The rain, omnipresent since he stepped off the plane, was again making a mottle of the silvery film of filth on the windowpanes. The sky had fallen so low that it almost sat on the Wall. The Wall that seemed to be the only horizon that Berlin could know, blinded the once-grand view from the hotel's entranceway. The wanton patterns of calligraphy scrawled on the Wall by truant citizens and over the wall by the hysterical flight of blackbirds, were effortlessly absorbed by the brute muteness of the gray concrete.

Just so had the worn red velvet of the interior absorbed and diffused the countless assertions of its transient inhabitants. Long before the hotel had been stranded and disenfranchised by the Wall, the pompous mock-baroque newness of this room had first been strained and stained by the imperial revels of raucous young Nazi officers exultant in the magnificence of their leader's design. Their defeat was all too democratically integrated in the musty perfume of neglect suffusing the room that was now host to the more victimless violence of art. Having long been abandoned to vandals, in the aftermath of the Reich's demise, the hotel had more recently been provisionally rehabili-

73

tated to serve the stage and the screen. The cavernous ballroom
was made to inhale the sweat and repetitious tedium of theater
rehearsals; and the bar where he stood was permitted a brief
comeback as a blaring and shabby disco in the latest film by one
of the most acclaimed of Germany's vanguard directors. Like
the film, the bar hadn't survived the director's desire to turn the
ever more convoluted fragmentation of his alienation into a new
wholeness motivated by old-fashioned love. The disco quickly
gave way to random disarray; makeshift tables and battered
folding metal chairs, styrofoam cups half filled with cigarette
butts, a motley assortment of overcoats draped in whatever
locations and configurations might give them hope of drying
out before their owners returned to them; wastebaskets brim-
ming over with crumpled papers and coffee grounds; electric
saws and drills; all crowned and barely lit by a hysterically askew
crystal chandelier. Producer's headquarters, news conference
room, cafeteria, and lounge for actors and actresses, coatroom
and storage space for the technical crew. Dust was the only
common denominator.

He was as confused as the room. He stared into the
bleak blankness outside, vainly conjuring up a vision that would
free him from the martyrdom to the plot he was commissioned
to construct. What urge had thrown him into servitude to
someone else's illusion? Why had he given up the hard-won
loneliness of his writing table to join in the confusion of this
collaboration with two others? How could he risk the blur of
triple vision, when his own was so hard to focus? To write for
actors with no roles instead of writing roles with no actors. And
then to maybe make it German. German, the language long
dormant in his brain that had begun making serious inroads into
his English. For, resist as he might, the increase in his German
vocabulary, achieved since his arrival, had taxed him with a
commensurate decrease in his English vocabulary, as though his

mind was only permitted to store a specific number of words. Worse, as he slowly started to think in German, he found it harder and harder to write in English. Now he stopped to make himself conscious of the language he was confused in; but he was interrupted by the touch more than the sound of a slight wheeze on the back of his neck. Without turning around, he knew immediately what body the breath belonged to. More palpable confirmation quickly followed, as he felt a hand slowly but firmly settle on his right shoulder. Exactly as he had dreamed it, seen it, and desired it every day since his entry into Berlin. The adrenaline that the hand injected into his system confounded the composure so necessary to the encounters he had previously witnessed. If he waited for his heartbeat to slow down, would the hand evaporate? He turned around. They were face to face. Then face in face, mouth in mouth. His tongue shed all the burdensome weight the German had added. The kiss was all there was. The blankness bloomed with surrender. Only slowly did the rancid vapors of brandy and cigarettes that he inhaled from the other mouth begin to sour the deliciousness of his daze and make the blankness bleak again. As consciousness began once more to rise to the surface, his tongue recoiled at the awareness of the hard, inorganic slipperiness of the roof of the mouth it had been probing, a repugnant plastic smoothness that obviously was a bridge holding false teeth in place. He withdrew his tongue and his surrender. He scanned the other's face coolly and almost cruelly, in search of the absences signaled by the alien prothesis. He saw too much of what he feared might be seen in himself. The golden tones of his desire had painted Carl's face far differently than the one he saw before him. He saw a face whose premature wrinkles told the story of excess' slow corrosion of elegance. He saw a mouth whose resoluteness was yielding to resignation. He saw slightly bloodshot eyes and nicotine-stained teeth and a sweat-stained shirt. Fantasies don't sweat. His kiss had turned the prince into a frog. Now the spell was broken and the story began.

He had been too surprised to take much umbrage at the sleaze gurgling under the soft-spoken sincerity of the producer's voice that invited him to Berlin. A voice that assured him that they were certain he could write for the stage; they knew he spoke German. The codirectors wanted him in Berlin immediately. It was superfluous to mention how famous the codirectors were. The play was already booked in some of the best houses in Europe and three theaters in America. As he was packing his bags, he found himself involuntarily reconsidering his disdain for the brokers of stardom and imagining himself being photographed and pinioned in the pages of *Vanity Fair*. Perhaps fool's gold was better than no gold at all. In the plane, his customary anxiety at being uprooted and suspended in the placelessness of the sky dissolved in the growing effluvium of anticipation.

At the airport, he was picked up by what he would soon realize was a generic Berlin female, a body whose contours were difficult to discern under layers of scruffy black, with a sallow face covered with enough makeup to almost hide a few late-blooming pimples and topped by a shapeless shock of acid, orange-red-brown hennaed hair that vainly protested the persistent grayness of Berlin's air. A swarm of these types, varying only slightly in height and width, attended to the more mundane functions of the production's progress. The driver handed him a bulging envelope and coolly explained that it contained the combined notions, not only of the two directors, but also of the two writers who had previously been engaged to chart and rechart the plot. On top, there was a note to him from some assistant insisting he translate into German a section of Polybius's *Histories* dealing with the destruction of Carthage by fire, as well as a nineteenth-century treatise on typhoid fever, both texts enclosed. Under these texts, he found a drawing of a fish with the inscription, "To RUDOLF, I LOVE YOU ALWAYS, E." There were also countless xeroxes of texts that included a phonetic translation of Hopi Indian chants, Goethe's ecstatically long description of a rock, a hilariously supercilious letter written by Maeterlinck, snippets from *Robinson Crusoe*, *King Lear*, *Oedipus Rex*, and *Walden Pond*, as well as reproductions of Caspar David Friedrich's precisely painted, yearning landscape voids; and at least fifty details of gesticulating hands, mostly of the Angel of the Annunciation or Buddha.

Was he to be a writer, or the accountant for two canni-bals of culture? Why hadn't he been informed that this plot had already swallowed and regurgitated two other writers? Why had he come to Berlin? Helplessly, he inquired who the Rudolf addressed in the fish drawing was. One of the two voided writers, she responded. His rampant Marxism had provoked several members of the West Berlin Senate, which was one of the major sponsors of the production. Questions about the misdoings of the second rejectee were cut short by their arrival at the rehearsal space. He was not to be permitted to first go to his hotel, nor to make a preliminary claim on some part of Berlin on his own. Doubly stung by jet lag and the contents of the manila envelope, he let himself be hurried into his indoctrination. His bleary eyes barely had time to register the hulking slab of the Wall that threatened to choke off what little air was permitted the crum-bling, shapeless monolith they were entering, a bloated form resembling some beached and barricaded whale.

Inside, he was steered through a cacophonous chorus of stagehands and actors and actresses in varying phases of dress and, then, into the vast, throbbing dampness of the rehearsal space. Here, he found himself effusively embraced by the long, lanky arms of a tall man with fiery eyes and cheeks. An abundant wreath of flattery, firmly and gently woven, quickly soothed his spinning head. This was the E. who had authored the fish drawing and inscription to the banished Rudolf. The embracer's alternating currents of vulnerable charm and fervid, evangelical eloquence were as disarming as legend had promised. Next to him stood a younger male, thinner, shorter, and wanly handsome but for his darting, reptilian eyes and perpetual squirm which made itself visible even under voluminous Japanese trousers and a baggy cashmere sweater. His remarkable cleanliness gave him the air of some hip android or of Barbie Doll's consort Ken dressed for an art stroll in New York's Soho. Ken was to be his name, just as E would be Svengali.

Ken and Svengali were the two directors that he was to collude with. Svengali had achieved a major reputation, in what some still referred to as avant-garde theater, by his creation and direction of exquisite tableaux that beguiled and bejeweled the premises of Artaud's theater with a moonstruck derangement. If his epic slow motion had a message beyond its self-entranced beauty, it seemed to be that all culture was a grievous crime against nature and that the end would never be soon enough. Ken had sprung fully formed from a television screen in Chicago. He was a talk show host whose studio set pulsed with a profusion of hula hoops, lava lamps, psychedelic posters, inflatable chairs, and any and everything Day-Glo or plastic that caught his retro eye. His willing victims joined in a sterilized burlesque of verbal insults and pie-throwing. Senators, fallen preachers, demoted captains of industry, high-profile divorcées, psychics, legitimate and illegitimate children of Hollywood stars, and an occasional mass murderer all anxiously sought to sate their unquenchable image thirst at the mirage of Ken's bubbling oasis. Beamed into living rooms around the world, his singular combination of androgynous coyness and redneck hostility made him almost everyone's favorite toy boy. The improbable union of Ken and Svengali had been fitfully brokered into consummation by the spectacle-obsessed producer. He offered Svengali his first taste of a mass audience, Ken some hope of intellectual validation, and the world another milestone in the deescalation of the cold war between high and low cultures. Profit and pop apocalypse for all.

How could he, the writer who had so scrupulously honed his saturnine skepticism, give words to this charade? Arrogance. His arrogance, at least as much as his confidence, convinced him his will would be done. And how could he not be seduced by the prospect of so many empty vessels anxious to be filled, and by the almost instant physical gratification of the stage, when all his writing, thus far, lay flattened on a page? Even on the first crazed day, he was struck by the wanton willingness of all the performers in this play. An energy all too easily construed as sexual doused him in a shower of erotic expectations. Almost all looked longingly at him, Svengali and Ken for the fulfillment of the roles that would make their life a possibility. These were to be his captors.

He had arrived in the middle of a break and was now passed around among the cast like the gleaming artifact of Americulture that he had been advertised as being. The leads were almost instantly apparent, not necessarily by their age or beauty, but more by their ability to hover and glide while, like fireflies, emitting a sporadic glow that flickered in the darkness of the inexperience they assumed surrounded them. The first to be noticed was a male of his own age. He was in the throes of reluctantly and involuntarily shedding the skin and stance of a younger life: lean and stringy, suavely blond and blue-eyed, with a rumpled elegance that mocked more than mimed the Aryan stereotype. He had the disconcerting mannerism of approaching people from behind and lithely laying a hand on the unsuspecting shoulder in front of him. And this is how he approached the new writer to proffer his name, Peter, and the thought that, till now, there were far too many trees in the play and not enough of him. Peter's jaded nonchalance and casual comic bent had earned him fame on German stage and screen but not in the roles he really craved. Hamlet would always elude him. He liked Peter and smiled as he watched him moving away while taking a furtive sip from the silver flask that never left his side, on the stage or in the street.

The other major players present were all female. One of a comically exaggerated lushness whose jubilantly cherubic face bobbed atop two breasts that might well have served as the dairy for a foundling home. She interrupted a magic trick she was performing for several technicians to offer him a bite of the outsized Bavarian pretzel on her prestidigitator's table. Then she passed him on to the lion-maned and -voiced vamp at her side. How could a production in Berlin be complete without a transvestite? This one was primarily famous for and known only by the English acronym that described the dilemma and/ or delight she was left in by the incompetence of her surgeon. Her voice, cloaked in a garish fake French accent, purred out the litany of her infamy: the doctor had only removed the c and o from her cock and added only the c, l, and i of her clitoris; and so she was made and named Click. Thus far, no one had proven her name to be a fraud. The other woman was clearly female but had made her reputation playing old men in eighteenth- and nineteenth-century comedies. On stage, her rasping voice as effortlessly roamed through senility as through all-knowingness. Offstage, she minced and condescended with Old World airs of highmindedness. She seemed born to bear the cross of culture. Varying faces and phases of androgyny rippled through the some twenty members of the supporting cast, mostly freshly matriculated dancers and thespians interspersed with some aging veterans and even a few amateurs. Most conspicuous was an older, balding man of rigid military bearing who thrust out his considerable stomach like a heraldic shield. German-born, Russian-accented, and incongruously called Herr Osborne. Missing and still not found in this motley crew was a young male lead, who, he learned, was to be a foil for Peter.

And so he came to Svengali (Ken was no longer in sight) seated at a long makeshift table covered with notes, books, and another frenzy of reproductions of art. Having asked him to sit down, Svengali immediately got up and sat in his lap. He would soon learn that this, like so many of the director's movements, gestures, and words, was not so much directed at or meant for the addressee as it was a rehearsal for an action that might end up on stage. Svengali talked about the play: what was important was the light, the light of destruction, the light of creation. There were to be ashes and darkness, a city in flames and a vast frozen plain, a forest, a factory, a dinosaur, a typhoid epidemic, a very old man (maybe some disenfranchised god) gurgling like a brook throughout the play; a mother, a whore, a tyrant (maybe a medieval sovereign, maybe a nineteenth-century robber baron), and his mirror image (maybe an idiot savant, maybe a downtrodden subject, maybe a long lost, bastard child). The tyrant/robber baron would seek salvation through his double but find it only after inadvertently causing the double's death. Shades of Oedipus, Moses, *The Prince and the Pauper*, Piaget's and Truffaut's *Wild Child*, and countless others flickered by as he gave yet another turn to his visionary kaleidoscope. Most of this would be resolved in this workshop and then go into real rehearsal (there would be four months in between to finish sets, costumes, and, of course, text). The break was over; the cast stopped its chatter and each resumed the last given place on the provisional stage. He watched with some surprise as a young actor his cruising eye had earlier dismissed as too effeminate assumed a potent, tensile grace molded by Svengali into the pose of a fox stalking a bird.

81

The fox sniffed, crouched, leaped, and snared the bird. Very slowly. Over and over and over again. And then one more time, but more slowly still. He listened and watched as three yards became first three miles, then three infinities. No action was too small or too inconsequential not to be cosmic. The afternoon session's repetitions went on for some four hours. He couldn't remember whether his watch was set to New York or to Berlin time. His resistance was dulled, his skepticism anaesthetized.

Once, maybe many times, he thought of getting up and leaving for the airport, only to find Svengali's hand on his arm. Then he would fall back into the mesmerizing rhythm of the fox's repetitions.

At the end of the day (what day he no longer knew), they took him to the room rented for him, handed him a bottle of vodka and more of Polybius to be translated. He had become as submissive as his typewriter. Ploddingly, he pounded his imperfect German onto the page. When he finally got up from this task, he barely noticed the meanness of his room and the unwanted narrowness of his bed; but, then, actual sex was simply not to be an issue here. He woke up thinking of Peter.

Like some houseless and hapless hermit crab, he slowly grew into the shell of the theater. Did he have any choice? The shades of difference between freedom of choice and the seemingly benign indoctrination into identification with his captors became too subtle to be significant. Every day but Sunday, he simply got up and went to the hotel that was called the theater, sat, watched, consulted with Svengali, and took notes. At the end of every day, Ken appeared from somewhere, simultaneously grinning and gritting his teeth; he would always be trailed by assistants and a girlfriend who smiled at everyone but spoke only to Ken, and then only in a barely audible whisper. Whatever had been done that day was run through for Ken; he took a few notes, nodded, frowned, and then withdrew with his entourage. The day was then officially over; but the cast milled around, reluctant to face the banalities of the street and anxious for the praise or the promise of more time on stage that Svengali would daily dispense to one or another of the chosen. Almost all were kept in a constant state of suspense as to who or what or how long they were to be.

Almost without exception, when he left the theater, he boarded first a bus and then a subway to one or another stop on the Kurfuerstendamm and then walked to the Paris Café for dinner—he could eat alone in comfort there and not worry about every dish being choked in cream and/or grease. There, he began taking notes on the notes he had taken in rehearsal. After his meal, he walked back to his cramped quarters through the rain that hadn't ceased since his arrival. As constant as the rain was an army of streetwalkers marching miniskirted and black-booted under gargantuan umbrellas: military mushrooms (sometimes poisonous) swelling up from the cracks in the pavement to thrive in the relentless dampness of Berlin. Otherwise he noticed only the Mercedes showroom. There all was dream, gleam, and dry.

In his room, he returned once more to note-taking and writing bits and pieces of monologue for the old man that were to alternately relieve and stress the catatonia being induced in the cast. Like everything else, the language to be heard had not yet been finally decided upon; he had not one but two languages that could threaten to clog up his pen. In English, he lost the tone. In German, he couldn't find the words. There was no word for "canyon" in German, but there were far more sonorous signifiers for the states of damp, such as *feucht* and *schwuel*. (Besides its reference to wetness, schwuel was still employed by some to furtively refer to homosexuality. A humid state of sexuality?). And so he wrote himself to sleep. In the morning he woke up thinking of Peter.

Even en route to the theater, all thoughts of another life were suppressed. Only two bus routes serviced the immediate vicinity of the theater and, given their remarkable punctuality, it was inevitable that he would find himself side by side with one or more members of the cast, after he rode the subway or bus. Most often he found himself awkwardly sifting around the domain of Herr Osborne's stomach as the aging actor chewed and spewed out the thick Russian *r*s that rumbled up from the depths of his diaphragm, *r*s that embraced the life story he was writing in between his acting roles. He claimed to have literally been born in the theater (during the third act of *King Lear*). He had spent thirty-eight years in Russia due to a false move at the end of World War II. In Russia, a new alphabet demanded the surrender of both his German and his English; he then was permitted to study with Stanislawski and became a semiprominent actor and director. In 1967, he was dispatched to Vietnam to direct a play called *Yankee Go Home*. Since his mysterious return to Germany, he had, due to his alien accent, always been cast as a Slavic émigré or army officer (the faces of his various roles were photo-collaged on the postcards he dispensed daily on the bus). Not surprisingly, he loved working with Svengali, because, with him, he didn't have to be a character actor. This bus opera came to an abrupt halt one day when Herr Osborne became vituperously anti-Semitic. The other passengers were less forthcoming; they usually included the sound technician, a Balinese dancer/actress, a diminutive retired female domestic, and a sublimely senile and lecherous old man with the frenetic grace of a silent movie comedian. These last two had been recruited from an old-age home. The old man's lyric lunacy made him the star of many a rehearsal break; he was far less applauded by the wardrobe assistants who had to deal firsthand with his incontinence.

The collaboration of captor and captive extended to all hours of the day and the night. If there was a break in his nocturnal note-taking, it was to sit in Svengali's hotel suite and ponder possibilities of plot and text. If he went out to a dinner party, it was one given by a member of the cast. If he went to a play or a movie, it was because some member of the cast had a role in it. Even in the co-ed sauna of the gym, where his body could almost lose Svengali, he once found himself squeamishly averting the blank stare of the deflated breasts of the actress who played old men.

On one such outing, he and several actors went to see a movie that starred both Peter and the famous actor who often received the roles that Peter always dreamed of playing. Berlin became the set for a love triangle in tones of a Germanic *Jules et Jim*. Peter, now called Carl, meandered melancholically through the streets of Berlin in search of the woman he and his friend had been enchanted by in the acrobatic act of a traveling circus. His slow roam always ended at yet another section of the Wall; he traversed the long street taken by the bus to the theater; he brooded aimlessly in the cafeteria of the National Library where cast members went for lunch, on those rare days they were given enough time. Finally, he ended up in the decrepit bar of the hotel itself—now transformed into a punky disco. Here his pilgrimage was rewarded with the sight of the missing acrobat. He approached her from behind. Like a butterfly, his right hand slowly fluttered to rest on her shoulder. The next morning, he woke up thinking of Carl.

Slowly, a skeleton of a plot was patched together, but one so intertwined with the ephemera and exotica of Svengali's hermetic mind, that all was afloat on a sea of ambiguity. Fire and ice, sapphire and topaz interrupted and temporarily blinded sequential ration. Was all the wall-building a reference to Berlin? Were the scars of typhoid a surrogate for the more contemporary plague of AIDS? Was the muttering old man one person or many, the father of the hero, or the hero in old age or in some afterlife? Would all the torn and crumpled paper, mock-props, and the wooden detritus pressed into service as town and forest really become bronze trees, malachite tables, a silver library, an armadillo head or a bird of paradise? What was the text to be? So far only snippets of appropriated writing and two of the short monologues for the old mutterer had any place. One day Ken's girlfriend gave forth with her only audible sentence, while watching the rehearsal's windup. Upon seeing the dinosaur that had just joined Svengali's bestiary, she shouted wildly, "Kiss the beast."

"Kiss the beast," shouted Svengali.

"Kiss the beast," chanted the cast, over and over again. "Kiss the beast" was threaded through the play.

Just as he was approaching the edge of depression and confusion as to what his writing role might be and how it might possibly satisfy him and Svengali too, he was asked to take several days off and compose a monologue for the hero. He was asked to write the beginning; but he chose, instead, the end; when the hero's double has died and he is seen roaming the wilderness in a stupor of delight, despair, and resignation to his own death. Thoughts of Carl fueled his writing, morning, noon, and night. He constructed a symphony of crazed regression: of childhood memories, of parental scorn, of nursery rhymes, of Shakespearean lines, of efforts to embrace the shadow of the dead double that was following the hero into the furnace of his mortality; of profound joy, of pain, of sonorous inconsequence. It was like nothing and like everything he had ever written before. He felt release for the first time since he boarded the plane for Berlin. He ignored the rain. He forgot that there had only been six hours of sunshine in all of November. He filled his room with flowers.

Carl took one look at his monologue and beamed with satisfaction at its length. Maybe now he would out-tower the trees. He left the rehearsal to study the lines on his own and returned an hour later to give his first recitation. Astoundingly, Carl read the piece almost exactly as it had been written and intended. His halting English only served to reenforce the zig-zagging fractures of his character's elegiac ending. Effortlessly, he pulled out all the stops of his nuanced range of emotion. The sinuous slump of his back faced the audience as all applauded his performance. Some time later, the producer snatched the still-beaming writer from rehearsal, took him to his office; and there, under the watchful stare of Ken, he oiled his way through his own monologue. The piece had been too long, the writing too ambitious for the nature of this project; they all had decided something more like contemporary song lyrics were in order here. Something like David Bowie . . . if only Malcolm McLaren had the time . . .

He felt the shell begin to crack. He felt a shock but no pain. He could say nothing; he fled the office. He stumbled into the bar. His gaze pierced the silvery grime of the huge windows in search of some resolution. He could not believe what he saw.

Storm Warnings

A fecal cloud began to roil his stomach and his writing space. The pungence was welcome. He turned into the gaseous drift to confront a vast puddle of a face emerging from a mass of rags. A figure without form, whose face had long ago given up all pretense of expression. It was left to the fetid folds of cloth to articulate whatever semblance of emotion might be necessary. He felt an unanswerable question beginning to gurgle up from those folds; but then the figure just turned and fluttered by.

There were not many, but still quite a few, homeless in the main reading room of the public library. It was huge and crowded and disarrayed enough so that their presence was more easily absorbed than in the far smaller and far more meticulously maintained art history reading room. There, guards were summoned as soon as a homeless dared to enter; the homeless was hastily ejected before smell could cloud the progress of scholarly quests. Of late he had begun to avoid the art history room.

He spent most of his time in the main reading room just floating in the limbo of half-remembered dreams or else trying to comprehend the rituals of that small tribe of the dispossessed whose members returned, like him, to the same seat day after day after day: the disheveled old crone who always sat transfixed in front of a volume of the encyclopedia opened to the entry for "crocodile." The fat balding man with the greasy red tie whose body was severely shaken and rattled by a coughing fit every other hour on the hour, who seemed to be devoting his life to encrusting the Zip Code maps of all the telephone directories with his nose pickings. The little woman with fading orange hair who, every time she finished a book, would surprise herself and those around her by wailing, "I still don't know who the Madonna of the Chair is." And so many more. Surely they all understood each other and had long rehearsed the plot they were part of.

He was meant to be reading a biography on the man idolized by the man he was meaning to write a biography about. Sharpening his autopsical skills. But it was winter, and the price of a bunch of arugula had risen and the taste declined and his mind was elsewhere. Maybe it was the sheer cold that had turned his wayward musings toward homelessness. Or was it the smells? If voyeur was the word for the sightsex-obsessed, what was the word for the smellsex-obsessed? Would it be olfacteur?

Smell, more than the other senses, was analogy-resistant. Its very specificity was utterly elusive and seemed to repel almost all the thrusts that adjectives could muster. Herbal, putrid, fruity, spicy, green, moldy, woodsy—seemed quite insufficient. Tuberose began to sound like its smell, but only fishy could really strike a nasal chord.

He continued to drift away from the disillusion of his work. Now into the realm of his heliotropic fantasies, to his summer sun, to the vulnerable defiance of the monarch butterflies drawn into wayward calligraphy around the sun by the will of the wind. To late August and early September, when he would lay on the beach and watch the monarchs write their serpentine, southward flight across the sky. And he would wonder whether their clustering glyphs were once again luring him with a decoy of meaning. What was certain was their determination to leave the waning sun of the Northeast for the more radiant warmth of Mexico's light. The burning orange, traced in black, of their wings was as powdery and fragile as pastel; but this fragility had the strength for a flight of some three thousand miles or more. And their migration seemed to stretch the length of their lives from the two-week span of other butterfly adulthood to as long as ten months. Their only baggage was the hormonal perfume they carried on their wings. Now millions of them would be hanging like a shifting, buzzing curtain of densely compressed light, from the trees in the village of El Rosario, west of Mexico City—settling to the ground with the setting of the sun. What was it like in El Rosario, how did their density smell?

It was February 9th. In the *New York Times*, "A Bronx man went berserk early yesterday when he discovered that the prostitute he had brought home was not a woman, the police said, fatally beating and stabbing the transvestite, then jumping to his own death as officers broke down his door." The previous February 9th he had been in India. There, in the *Mahabarata*, Krishna dressed himself as a woman and made himself available to the still-virginal firstborn son of Arjun as he was going into battle.

He used to scan the entire *New York Times* in counterpoint to the bronchial rumble of the subway, on the way to the library. Of late, he scanned more selectively if at all. News like "sperm cells possess the same sort of odor receptors that allow the nose to smell, suggesting that sperm navigate toward a fertile egg by detecting its scent...", he would tear out and save. Mostly he would furtively look for one of those cars largely abandoned but for four or five anomalous hovels of cloth that sheltered the homeless. Then he would sit and slowly release himself into the hypnotic violence of the smells. If he could think at all it was to ponder whether the fabric layers cloaking the homeless were formed by the shape of the body they enveloped or whether it was the fabric that was shaping the body inside. Occasionally he missed his stop; but always, by the time he got off the subway, his nose had become oblivious to the smell. When had smell evaporated into the memory of smell? Wondering why so many politicians were reputed to have a preference for oral sex, he followed his steps to the library.

He could not remember when the homeless had started to claim such prominence in his consciousness. Even less could he remember when it was that he began to find them valiant? When was it that the stark fact of their continued existence became a kind of heroic deed? Their aimless drift in subway currents began to take on a certain grace. The entranced way they fluttered by. They were not violent. Their smell seemed to protect them from most predators. Perhaps it was the culture's abhorrence of aimlessness that made so many commentators claim that two-thirds of the homeless populations was mentally impaired and/or drug addicted. Wouldn't they be truly subversive if they had freely chosen their path? Maybe it was their embodiment of the smells that so many millions of dollars were spent on to suppress. The furious gases they were so often enveloped by failed to arouse the prerequisite shame in them. He began to think of the homeless as a kind of avant-garde, deep condensations of what was repressed.

For so much of his own life he had often been denied or had denied himself the sense of smell. He began to wonder what his relentless smoking might have to do with the subversion of his nose's powers. Winter alone wasn't responsible for clogging up his nostrils. He couldn't blame it all on his grandmother who had so long ago made him constantly and pitilessly scrub all the soulful parts of his body. He could hardly recall that time, in his childhood, before order had banished odor, when he had so indiscriminately pursued all smells—between his toes, in his crotch, behind his ears, on the chairs recently vacated by his parents' guests, anywhere at all.

He forgot where he learned that schizophrenics could smell the moods of others. That they themselves can give off different odors at different times. Did these odors create accompanying personalities? As their biochemical imbalance is heightened, so too is their odor. Some, particularly those with delusions of sexual change, have smell hallucinations. He wondered what the difference in smell of a transsexual before and after might be.

In the library, he learned that the word for the hormone secreted to exert sexual attraction, pheromone, was coined in 1959. Pheromones were first thought to belong only to insects, then to fish and birds, and were finally attributed to humans. Pheromones can be found in urine, among other places. They are resistant not only to analogy but to allegory.

Desire by Numbers

Bring me chocolates not lies. My doctors give me enough lies, my visitors don't have to. Why can't I have something smooth and creamy and truthful?

I'm not lying. I'm trying . . .

Trying to forget something, and it's not something more important to forget than to remember. You've forgotten the real reason for your story. What is it that's lurking behind your words?

I'm just trying to continue where we left off the last time I visited you.

Sure. Sure. So you've got a captive audience and you have another twenty minutes before they kick you out. So go on. You were just about to call out for sex. It was hard to understand, but maybe only a writer would choose a hustler by his voice. Was that it? Go on. Start again. Where does this begin?

On the phone. A recording. "Press 6 to hear the actual voices of New York's finest professionals and how you can meet them." Amidst the repetitive profusion of bubble butt, nine inches uncut, forty-eight-inch chest, twenty-nine-inch waist, all-American bodybuilder, blond blue-eyed hunk, stone-hard muscles—especially the one that counts, you won't regret it, pure Italian, swimmer's build, horse-hung black Romeo, you might have seen me last night on the *Robin Byrd Show*, there came a voice less preposterous, less boastful, even a bit self-mocking. I dialed that voice's number.

Were you horny?

No.

So, you wanted something else.

No, no, I wanted him. I wanted to see him.

You wanted to see a voice.

I wanted him.

It's too soon to ask why. Just go on.

I hung up the phone. The voice called back to make sure I wasn't a hoax and then promised to arrive in half an hour. My heart began to pound. What if he was just a petty criminal, maybe even violent? I hid my wallet. I realized my nervousness would make it difficult to get a hard-on—that made me more nervous. The buzzer rang. Should I answer it? I felt a tremor about to rupture my speech. I opened the door trying to smile coolly. Hi, don't look at me like that, I'm glad you called me, where's the bedroom, I'll give you a massage first. I felt the first surge of blood thickening my cock. Would I be able to maintain it?

So your cock and your voice rise and fall together. But what about him? What made him right? Where does this begin?

What made him so right was that he was so unremarkably attractive. There was nothing about him physically that I can now remember, except that he had black hair and very clear brown eyes. Even his cock was dutifully average but very quick to spring into hardness. Later he told me his erections were encouraged by liberal doses of some pill he took. His voice was pleasing but without any intonation or mannerism that might locate it geographically. His name was harmless and free of almost all associativeness. John was his name, if that was his real name. I thought he would probably be perfect. Had he been any more particular, more striking, even slightly eccentric in speech, he might have become too demanding, maybe too forcefully underlined the jarring disparity in our ages.

Does being over fifty really make illusion so much more fragile that you can only fantasize about the attainable? And how could you not have asked about those pills? We still haven't begun. What do you really remember?

" . . . and when your affections are not too involved, you give much better value for the money." I remember that from *The Snows of Kilimanjaro*. He had given value. Not the greatest sex I ever had, but value nonetheless. Don't make me discount that. I did lose my hard-on but came anyway and then came again—and then it was really hard. Afterward my body vibrated with the delirium John's hands had drawn all over it. It was an illusion, yes; but just for a moment not so fragile. Just for a moment I thought I was shaking sunlight from my hair. I felt like those ancient Roman banqueteers who feasted on golden plates, then threw those plates through the windows into the Tiber, knowing full well that there were nets to catch them. And weren't these lies better than the cruel truths of daylight?

Your illusion is still only halfhearted. Perhaps it would have been more courageous had the plates been fake. And didn't you ever wonder what John was imagining so he could maintain the pill-induced erection that was gold-plating you? I know you're not yet ready to answer that, so just tell what you felt after John left.

After he left, I sat stunned at my desk. I couldn't believe that I had actually done it. I'd never done it before—never paid for it.

That's what they all say. Do you really expect me to believe it this time?

That's up to you.

All right. Go on being stunned.

I can't be, if you keep interrupting me.

Go on.

Well, I was confused. I thought I was meant to feel

demeaned, but I didn't. I couldn't get his phone number out of my mind. I hadn't even tried to memorize it, but it just hovered there like some insect that had buzzed into the room and wouldn't go away. It just perched somewhere beyond my reach. I knew I would call again.

Then I felt myself drifting into one of those waking dream states. Aimlessly I opened the top desk drawer and was greeted by the dead monarch butterfly that, some time ago, I had placed in the compartment for my pens and pencils. The black tracery on its burnt orange and white-dappled wings still seemed to be recording the evolving patterns of its growth. But the velvetiness of its fluffy black body suddenly reminded me of Peter. Peter had never tired of describing the silky black velvet down that crowned the dicks of the young boys in the sex clubs and circuses of Bangkok—very different, he said, from the crinkly curls of the seaweed cascading over the top of adolescent Japanese dicks. Peter had started an album of pubic hairs which he carried with him on his frequent travels, in constant search of new specimens. I had never been permitted to see its actual contents nor had he answered the many queries about the means of his acquisitions. But often I tried to envision the unruly silken curls and wiry coils feverishly springing across pages, tracing the trajectory of Peter's wayward passions. A perfect travel diary, written in a language all could understand.

But where is John? What happened to John? Why is Peter replacing him? What did Peter do? Why is your narration so unreliable? Where does this begin?

Peter had fallen in love with Number 9 at the Joy Bar in Bangkok, although he and Number 9 had been entangled for only an hour or so in the fluorescent magic of one of the many cubicles behind the bar. For years he never stopped raving about Number 9, the boy of joy. Nubile, warm, and slippery, mystifyingly acrobatic, endlessly accommodating but constantly in the lead, a serpent's tongue capable of wrapping itself around his erection, a mouth as thick and sensual as a pre-Khmer Vishnu, black eyes that shot out sparks of laughter, and a long, pointed penis that remained rock-hard for the duration of their encounter—these are but a partial catalog of Peter's ecstatic words. Even as he lay in the hospital with his skin so tightly drawn around his shriveling frame that his rib cage was about to break through and his skin's near transparency was festooned with Kaposi's polka dots, Peter still raved about Number 9. Number 9, he was quite certain, had been the groom of his demise; but, as long as he could still talk, he talked about this boy of joy with tears of joy in his eyes. He died with the Number 9 on his lips.

Peter did what you couldn't do. He left you with your halfhearted desire, but you, at least, were alive. How did Peter leave? Where did this begin?

Peter left me in India, in the state of Kerala, in a state of high excitement. We had spent a number of days in Khajuraho stoned and enraptured by stone, basking in the lavish glow of Hindu sexspirituality. There, some twelve or so medieval temples in the form of staggered phalluses rise up from terraced bases and are completely encrusted with an undulating orgy of curves richer and juicer than any tropical fruit, lusher and more languid than the petals of a lotus. In lavish slow motion, hundreds upon hundreds of couples and groups fuck and fellate in a never-ending polyphony of positions. So excessive is the torrent of curves that it becomes overpoweringly silent and sublime. One of the temples was abutted by a small pool, and there the water's rippling reflectiveness turned the stone back into soft, undulating flesh. I remember Peter bending over the edge of the pool to fleetingly send his reflection into this perfection.

And what about Peter? Wasn't Peter's reflection perfection, too? Surely you haven't forgotten how beautiful Peter was.

No, I haven't, but we were just friends.

So being "just friends," you were naturally oblivious to his beauty. Or were you just forcing yourself to blur his reflection?

No. No. Why would I do that? Why do you keep trying to divert the course of my story?

To help you find the right path, since you don't seem to know the way. So go back. Go back to the temples. What happened when you turned away from all that beauty?

We were face to face with a decrepit vendor—one of those sorts whom time has driven back into bulbous, infantile androgyny. He whimpered and sneered and shook fistfuls of postcards reproducing what we had just seen.

Another merchant of dreams. Are they all representations of you? Who is selling and who is buying? Why can't this be clearer? What did the vendor do?

If you know so much, why don't you tell the story?

No. No. Not this part. Not the vendor. Go on, please. What about the vendor? Where does this begin?

With his eyes darting ceaselessly from Peter's crotch to mine, he counted up, in nasal singsong English, the number of couples he had recently spied having sex in the mango grove behind the place where he stood. Then, in conspiratorial whispers, he told us of three temples dedicated to the homosexual deity Ayuppa, outside of Trivandrum, not far from where the sacred elephants were kept. There, he maintained, the churning stone that embraced the temples was exclusively male. For an instant, he pulled out a photograph too distressed by time to reveal more than a spectral chorus of outsized cocks. A generous tip elicited no further information and only vague directions with assurances that the path would become clear from the pond where the elephants were bathed and groomed. The idea of the temples was so fabulous, we hardly knew whether to believe him. Maybe he'd been eavesdropping on our nightly fantasies since our arrival in Khajuraho. Nonetheless, we made immediate plans to leave for Trivandrum. Ceaselessly we hummed: Ayuppa, Ayuppa, Ayuppa.

Please, let me take my medication before you have an epiphany. Where are you going? You're moving too far away. You never finished John. What about John, what about your amorphous hustler and your amorphous desires? Why won't you focus?

All right, All right. John. You won't try to understand. I really wanted John. I simply needed John. Now let me go on.

No. You needed John only because you were scared to imagine something better. Peter may have ended up with Kaposi's sarcoma, but he imagined Kama Sutra. He was careless. His end is horrible, but your beginning is insipid.

Whose story is this anyway? Why can't I tell it?

Because you are not a reliable narrator. There is no precision in your subterfuge, no shape to your ambiguity. You are trying to give form to an empty dream. Try again. What about John? We know John is in the past tense, now, but what did John do to displease his john?

Nothing, really. Nothing. I know, I know why I was doing it. I've already admitted that my ego needed massaging more than my dick. Isn't that what I'm supposed to elaborate on?

No, no. You're giving me explanations when narration is called for and narration when explanation is called for. Excuse the bad pun, but just stick to John for a moment. What happened to John?

John was good. He was performing perfectly. But one day, when I called, the voice on the answering machine introduced itself as "Juan." He still let me call him John but said his real name was Juan. His favorite uncle's death had triggered a return to his Ecuadorian roots as well as a desire to revive his lapsed acting career. So many of them are failed actors or junkies. I guess I was lucky he wasn't a junkie. He wanted me to listen to the lines he was rehearsing for an audition. It was a romance; his lines sounded too much like what he had been saying to me. I couldn't stand it.

So what do we have now—two bad directors or two bad actors? You couldn't stand someone else directing your voice.

No. It was just so ordinary all of a sudden.

Ordinary. That's your most accurate word so far. Now we're getting closer to the beginning. Ordinary. Nothing withers the erotic faster than the ordinary. The erotic thrives on danger, the alien, the exotic, the unknown. You foreclosed on Eros's territory from the start. So now that we've left John/Juan on someone else's stage, tell me about the real image pressing your narrative on its zigzagging path. What flesh is buried in your reveries on stone? Aren't those boys in Bangkok the illusion you really wanted to hold? Aren't they the ones you'd like to have dancing in your pupils?

No. No. That's your idea. You are turning this into another story. I can't do that.

Yes. Yes. Cannot and want are not mutually exclusive. What about your angel of the sitar? Why have you been hiding him?

I'm not hiding him. It was something that just happened.

Sure. Sure. But tell it anyway.

I've already told it.

Not here. Go on. Let yourself go a little. Where does it begin?

In the hotel in New Delhi. There were musicians playing in the restaurant. The one on the sitar looked like a tawny young Bacchus. Caravaggio couldn't have painted him any better. His eyes and full mouth smoldered with a sensuality that ignited the luster of his face. He kept smiling at me. The slippery drone his fingers drew from the strings started to vibrate in my groin. I got a hard-on. I was really agitated. He kept smiling at me. I left the table and went to the men's room. I just stood and stared at myself in the mirror, trying to deny the evidence of time's cruel sculpture. My lips had been thinned and my smile ever more cramped by the deepening clamp that curved out from my nostrils and closed in hard on the far edges of my mouth.

The door opened and he glided in, still smiling and now humming like his sitar. My drumming heart leapt into a thumping accompaniment. He stood by my side and we stared at ourselves and at each other in the mirror. So still and concentrated we stood that I could see the reflection of his reflection glistening in the darks of my eyes on the surface of the glass. We looked for a long, long time. Finally he said, "Now I see you as you are," and he turned and flowed out of the room on the tide of his loose garment's gossamer drapes.

That's not the way you ended it the last time . . .

That's the way I remember it.

No. The last time you recounted that he shed his clothes and coiled himself around you slithering all over your body, softly hissing and licking your greedy limbs. And you came just before he reached your cock. And you seemed to imply that as you came, another reflection took its place beside yours. Who is the bearer of that reflection? You're still hiding too much.

No, I'm not. That's not true. It didn't happen.

There's still no focus here. Your deeds, when you remember them, sound like they've been stolen from a book; and then you rip them up. Why can't you just grab an ass, suck a dick, smell a crotch, let some shit ink your fingers? At least tell me how old you think this sitar-strumming vision was.

Maybe fifteen. I don't know. What difference does it make?

A lot of difference. Maybe you could end by beginning in Bangkok. There you could really exercise your demigodly prose. Under cover of Asian exoticism, you could become Zeus snatching Ganymede under his eagle wing and carry youth to some Olympian grove. Your words could become more courageous, your thoughts more perilous. You could be Apollo stripping and oiling your body to wrestle with Hyacinthus. Only this time, don't throw a discus, or you'll kill him again and have to write his name on another flower. What about Orpheus after he lost Eurydice for the second time? Maybe Orpheus suits you best. Like him, you could sing with your lyre about the tonic joys of fine, hairless boys with skin as flawless and smooth as translucent travertine. Or with a furious leap of your imagination you might just picture their form as being made of human flesh.

I don't understand. Why all this mockery now?

To draw your mouth closer to your desire.

Now who is hiding his memory? Who spent all those hours in praise of Greece's homosexualized mythology? Who kept asking "Where is our *Iliad*, where is the book we can build our culture on?" So now where is your *Iliad*?

On cardboard coffee cups. Forget the gods. Get back to the boys. Tell me about the one that followed you into the shower at an indoor pool and wanted to blow you in exchange for some dollars? Was that in Moscow or was it Berlin? And what about that Puerto Rican angel whose name actually was Angel, who called you Daddy and wanted you to piss on him and punish him and call him a pig and fuck him with your black leather jacket on, while he moaned on and on about what a bad son he had been?

No. That never happened. This isn't my story. You're changing too much.

All right, All right. The pose can't be forced. Return to your stated path. You and Peter were going to Trivandrum to take a communion of writhing stone thighs. Where does it begin?

We hired a car and drove to the elephant reserve. Some thirty or forty of them were tethered to thick posts, and waiting to be fed huge bails of hay or to be walked to a pond where they sucked immense quantities of water into their trunks and showered themselves while an attendant scrubbed them down. They were as docile and smiling as puppies. They were as light on their feet as dancing balloons. We watched their airborne prance and play so long we almost forgot why we were there. When we started to ask about the temples, the attendants shrugged or smiled or shook their heads or held out their hands for tips that yielded muteness. None of them would speak. One looked right through us with a troglodytic stare and pointed to an elephant who, while he was being scrubbed, slowly sprouted a glaring pink erection far taller and fatter than my whole body. Dutifully we scrutinized the elephant's gray parchment skin as though the thousands of wrinkles etched into its surface might somewhere reveal a map that would point us on our way. Finally, Peter whispered, "This elephant is the only temple we are going to see," and slowly pulled me back to the car. I couldn't speak. We never mentioned Ayuppa again.

So now your tongue turned to stone. What was it you wanted to take from those temples? What buried hopes did you want unearthed? What role did Peter play? What was it that cracked in Trivandrum? Why did Peter leave for Bangkok? Why did you let him leave?

He was leaving for Bangkok anyway. I knew that. I told you that.

There's something panicky in your voice now. Can you hear it?

No. I only hear your aggression. You're pushing me in the wrong direction.

So what direction were you going in, when you left Peter?

I didn't leave Peter. He went to Bangkok, I went to Australia. To the Great Barrier Reef. I was going to scuba dive.

Oh no. Were you thinking of casting your prose on flowing water so it might become still more elusive?

No. Let me go on. Your inquisition is becoming blind. Underwater there is no prose, no weight, no smell, only sight. I had to go.

All right. Go on. Where does it begin?

Under the surface. The surface was uncustomarily becalmed and bejeweled by the sun. On the surface I floated in circles of jade. Underneath, all was movement. Some like fluid flora, some like throbbing viscera, all the corals that turn to cold stone when exposed to the air pulsed underwater in stunning variations of gelatinous luminosity as capable of unfurling in yards of starched lace as protruding from the sea bottom like the buried antlers of a silver stag or giving body to the spectral coruscations of an X-ray of the brain. Sea anemones swirled their tentacles of mauve transparency as though to conduct this soundless phantasmagoria into a crescendo that I could never know the orchestration of. Day after day after day, I was suspended in their liquid, lunar grotto, surrounded by colonies of fish so vivid and radiant it seemed as though someone had spilled them out of a jewelry box. The shifting bottom was blurring and seemed insubstantial; more substantial was the plane of my liquid, mirrorlike ceiling. And it was toward this ceiling that my unstable buoyancy was being urged. Slowly top and bottom became reversed, and I felt I was turning inside out.

Now the image is finally becoming clearer. But what did you dream once gravity had returned your body's weight?

What more could I dream than what I saw?

Peter. Peter. Wasn't Peter flowing through your dreams? You dreamed of Peter all the time. I know you were dreaming of Peter.

Now whose voice has panic grabbed? You keep pushing Peter into my story.

You dreamed of Peter.

Yes I dreamed of Peter. I dream of Peter every night. Peter's mouth emerging slowly from a calla lily and singing a song that I can never hear when I wake up. I can only remember calla lilies.

Stop. Stop. Don't retreat now. Don't use flowers as an alibi.

No, you stop. It's your jealousy that keeps warping my reflections. You, you love Peter.

Yes. I love Peter, and so do you.

Yes.

So how does this begin?

I can't remember anymore.

Popeye's Demise

I was as embarrassed to be squirming as I was by the cause of my squirming. My father was the cause. Not only was my father wearing a ridiculous old-fashioned, two-piece bathing suit; but, also, he was not Popeye. It was as easy to see that he wasn't Popeye as it was hard to accept. For the previous five years, which added up to more than half of my life, I had only known my father as Popeye.

The image of my father as Popeye, together with the English language, had been thrust upon me just at that moment when the glutinous porridge of German that I had been born into and out of, no longer stifled my tongue. At that very moment Popeye and English laid siege to my consciousness, and my tongue was once more oppressed with trauma and stutter. It was not long, of course, and, of course, I couldn't remember how long, before I so totally identified with my new captors that I became one with them and they with me. English and Popeye together structured my new life.

I was just four and only just starting to have my first remembered thoughts of being when my father, whose image was not nearly as well formed in my thinking as that of my mother, disappeared. So too the vast house only photographs would remember, the maid, the gardener, and my nurse, all of whom left no trace whatsoever, and the German shepherd whose cold nose would rub against my thoughts for the rest of my life. All, and then some, were replaced by a large apartment in a large, red-brick apartment house on a well-tended knoll overlooking the railroad tracks and the Hudson River that flowed alongside them. The entire apartment house, but for the apartment shared by my mother, my grandmother, my brother, and myself, was filled with English. There were many dogs, but not one German shepherd. And there were quite a few children of or near my own age, all of whom showed signs of dismay and astonishment that I could not understand them.

No explanation was given to me for my father's disappearance. None. One day my mother handed me a sheet of paper and said, "This is from your father." The paper seethed with clusters of pointy lines that flustered through two-thirds of the page. The bottom third of the page was undisturbed in whiteness except for the lower right corner that was inhabited by a rubbery, modular male figure stretching his hilarious anatomy into a wave and a smile. The bulbous head was topped by an all-too-small sailor's cap, not unlike the one occasionally seen on some of the children in my new environs. The sailor stood on a fragment of a sailboat's prow, in the middle of a wash of limpid blue. The word "priapic" was certainly not to be found in the still tiny inventory of my English, but I was immediately drawn to this jocular form.

Nor was the character Popeye known to me. Even after my full indoctrination into English, which was still some time away, it would be still some more time before the characters of America's mass media would have any opportunity to interact with my own character. And then, Popeye would be joined by Olive Oyl, Wimpie, et al., in tales of raucous pugilism; whereas, now he appeared, week after week, after week, in splendid and iconic isolation on the lower right-hand corner of the page. Always in some form of greeting. Always by or in the blue of the sea. Always, just for me. At the end of every day, when my mother returned from work, I longed for her to say, "Here, this is from your father," almost as much as I longed for the hug and the kiss and the sweet smell of lipstick dispensed immediately upon her entrance into the apartment. After months of my mother's once-a-week, "Here, this is from your father," this is from your father became this is your father. And so it was.

What was on the rest of Popeye's page ? "What's that?" I asked my mother. "Your father's writing," she said. "Huehnerschrift," my grandmother said. None of this answered my question. My hand, my mind, and my language were still in the formative stages of their partnership; and my own efforts at writing still shuddered with confusion. Vowels and consonants had yet to be filled with the sound of the spoken words they combined to represent. And there was much interference on the circuits that ran from my mind to my right hand. My letters were defensively bold and had a tendency to stray. Even though my acquisition of spoken English seemed to be proceeding quite automatically, the "the" and "cat" my mother gently coaxed me to copy remained, for the moment, quite abstract. Nonetheless, my letters had a kind of discrete form, whereas my father's flew together in a jagged and formless discursiveness that held out little hope of meaning. Mostly, my father's writing looked like windswept wavelets that seemed to mean to form the seaborn Popeye's background. And so my father's writing remained, even after there was no longer Popeye inhabiting the lower right corner of the page. My own writing slowly acquired sound and sense; but my father's writing, without Popeye, became as inscrutable as the glyphs of a culture I had no part in. Only my mother was able to comprehend it; to me, it would remain indecipherable for the rest of my father's life.

Now the new figure of my father stood in front of me and provided none of the comfort and familiarity that had so freely flowed from Popeye. He even seemed to be trying to subvert Popeye. When my father was alone with me, he spoke to me in German, while Popeye had, for some time now, been waving to me and smiling at me in English. Since when I couldn't remember. Nor could I remember when I had started dreaming in English. What intimacy I was capable of could only happen in English; German now had a hard shell I could barely penetrate. German would always remain the language of the four-year-old being I no longer was. I wished my father would speak English to me in private, and German in public; but that, of course, was not really possible. Popeye, at any rate, would continue to enter my dreams in English.

I could see the others looking at my father—not so much at him as at the anachronism of his two-piece bathing suit. I could see the grownups looking discreetly and quickly turning away, then looking again, when my father wasn't looking their way. Those my own age or older looked more brazenly, some snickered and pointed; one came up and asked me, "Why is your grandfather wearing a bathing suit like that?" "He's not my grandfather," was the only answer I could muster. Not only was my father wearing a two-piece bathing suit; but he was, indeed, also old enough to be my grandfather. And his skin was very white, when everyone else's had the bronzed glow of summer ease. It wasn't even the reassuring white of Popeye's sailor suit.

My father's eyes seemed to bulge in their struggle for sight through the thick lenses of the glasses he wore. And this seeming bulging, as well as his partial baldness that, due to the premature grayness of his remaining hair, appeared, at first sight, almost total, were the only features he might be said to share with the awkward but engaging lumpiness of Popeye's features. But, in the end, there simply was no getting around the fact that the figure of my father and the figure of Popeye were not at all related. And how was I now to relate to the one, or to the other?

The excruciating saga of my father's two-piece-bathingsuitedness was being enacted on the manicured lawn surrounding the large swimming pool of the country club that lay walled in, like an enchanted castle atop a hill, and ruled more than overlooked the apartment house where I lived and the neighboring variants of neo-Georgian and neo-Tudor strivings for English exclusivity.

The only positive aspect I could attribute to the new figure of my father was that with him came access to the Edenic enclosure containing the swimming pool I had for so long longed to have access to. But my pleasure in the aquamarine expanse rippling at my feet was all but erased by the jarring appearance of the alien genie who had made my wish come true. For three years, my mother had patiently but laboriously fended off my litany of pleas to gain entrance to this pool; she had tried, in vain, to explain that the expense of the country club was beyond her reach. For a while, after my thinking had become almost totally English and the children of my age had no further reason to deride my incomprehensibility, I had been invited to the pool by a boy of my own age, who was imbued with a blue-eyed blondness and gentle but willful recalcitrance very much like my own.

Tad was his name, and he not only had parents who were members of the country club; but he also had a cocker spaniel puppy who became the agent of our friendship. Unaided by grownups, Tad and I determined to teach each other to swim. And we did. And my body slowly found a grace it would not be able to find on land, for some time to come. It found much more besides.

It was from Tad I learned that my uncircumcision rendered me unlike most other boys. My grandmother had convinced me that my penis was a foul agent in need of constant cleansing. "Wasch dein Schlingel," my grandmother chanted nightly. "Wasch dein Schlingel." Customarily, my eyes avoided all contact with my penis, except when I pissed or cleaned myself under stern grand-maternal promptings. I automatically extended the same avoidance to Tad's penis, whenever we were changing in the locker room, on the way to the country club pool. One day, Tad turned me around and said, "yours is really funny; look at mine, I have no skin over it." Tad then reached down and gently not harshly like my grandmother, pulled back the foreskin and began to softly massage the emergent head with his thumb and forefinger. Tingling spasms raced through my body and became all but unbearable as Tad's fingers began to rotate around the sensitive red rim of my head. "My father does this to me, you do it to me too," said Tad. The sudden clatter of footsteps spelled an end to my astounded arousal. We jumped into our swimming trunks; and, as we descended to the pool, Tad asked, "The war's over, where's your dad?" I wanted to answer, "On the lower right corner of the page;" but I just said, "Away."

Not long thereafter, Tad told me that his mother was taking him and the cocker spaniel back to Arizona. The idyll of the pool was abruptly over, and I returned to my reclusiveness. Sometimes, the astringent vapors of chlorine would be wafted down the hill to tease my nostrils with narcotic promises that turned Tad into currents of aquamarine. These currents were quickly swept away by my grandmother's relentless cleanliness. When she wasn't preparing meals or tending the small vegetable garden she had claimed from a patch of nearby, undeveloped land, she marched me in and out of the bathroom or to the schoolbooks she herself could not read and did not trust. Somewhere, she had procured a slim book, in German, that had frozen on its cover, a young boy whose every hair stood rigidly upright on his head. His arms were just as rigidly extended; and, from each finger of his outstretched hands, dripped perfectly shaped, pointed droplets of red. Struwelpeter was his name and the title of the cautionary tale that filled the book. Struwelpeter lived in constant fear of the giant scissors wielded by the local tailor. Scissors that would punish his hands and fingernails, if they were not kept constantly clean. To every knock on his door, Struwelpeter faintly replied, "Enter, if you're not a tailor." "Herein wenn es kein Schnedier ist" would ring through much of my youth and echo even into my adulthood.

The abbreviation of grandmother commonly used in German is "Oma," and I loved the softness of that name as much as I feared the gardening-callused hands that extended from it. "Oma, Oma, Oma," I softly chanted to myself. "Oma," I would hum while I sneaked into the hallway closet to caress the head of my grandmother's fox stole and play with the spring that had replaced the fox's jaw so that it might hold its tail in place when the fox was draped around my grandmother's ample bosom, on those rare occasions when she got dressed up. The fox would be accompanied by a tall, brimless, black felt hat, like a pot without its handle, sitting staunchly on disciplined waves of yellow-gray hair that were ordered once a week by the heated tongs of a curling iron. The donning of hat and fox almost always meant church. By herself, my grandmother had found a Lutheran church, an hour's walk away, where she journeyed every Sunday to strengthen her vows of cleanliness and the righteous condemnation of her absent son-in-law whom she had thus far only known for the first three months after her arrival in America. Popeye meant nothing to her. Nor did the endearment Oma, which was indeed alien to her Spartan sturdiness.

When I was alone in the apartment, and that was very often, I liked best of all setting my eyes free to float and bob on the intricate, symmetrical arabesques of tendrils and floreate forms that had been so wondrously and meticulously woven into the silky softness of the Oriental carpet that transformed the living room floor into an enchanted forest. Sapphire blue and pale, China blue urns and vases bursting with swaying fronds of dusty pink and moss green; delicate ferns unwinding their coiling stems of crisply pointed leaves; free-floating arching branches heavy with full lotus blossoms or bristling with the myriad buds of some still secret species of flower—all unfurling in their preordained order from the ground's deep red that was so much richer and more fertile than that of any garden my grandmother might tend. I would start at the panoply of borders, where the repetitive rhythms were slower, traveling around the periphery until my eyes were accustomed to the glowing darkness, and then spill my gaze into the tumult of red. My eyes would race and roll from medallion to medallion, from blossoms to buds, from blue to gold to green, in my anxious desire to possess it all at once. Only slowly would the totality of the design rise to the surface and await the calmer caress that grows from more measured sight. For silent hour upon silent hour, I wove myself into the obsessive completeness of the carpet.

It was on the carpet that I first saw my father when he returned. Big, black, shiny wing tip shoes with thin leather laces appeared one day, out of nowhere, in the lower right of the carpet's plane. So engrossed had I been in my botanical musings that I hadn't heard the shoes enter; nor, at first, could I look at the body connected to them. Automatically I tried to integrate the pointed, perforated pattern added to the surface of the shoes into the carpet's linear patternings. But their symmetries were incompatible. Finally I looked up into the implacable face that was speaking to me in German, the language I now only spoke to my non-English-speaking grandmother, in our curt exchanges. "Ich bin dein Vater," announced the figure with the wing tip shoes. Neither kiss, nor hug, nor touch of any sort was risked. The next day we were together at the country club pool; neither one of us was any more comfortable than we had been upon our initial remeeting. I missed Popeye. I wondered who my father was. I couldn't remember having actually seen him before. Altogether, I remembered very little of anything that had transpired in my life before.

On my previous visits to this pool, I had always avoided the high diving board. Even after I had learned to totally give in to the water's embrace and move with it rather than against it, the thought of jumping, to say nothing of diving, from so high up, into that embrace, cramped my body with fear. Once, when Tad and I were the only children there, I had climbed the ladder and, inch by inch, inched my way toward the end of the board. When the railing that met the ladder at the top of the stairs came to an end and the diving board's resiliency began to spring with the pressure of my cautious steps, my feet simply protested and refused to move any closer to the perilous edge. I tried not to look down; but, when inevitably I did, I was rocked by vertigo. I was certain I would fall and break, like a sheet of glass, into a thousand splintered shards that would disappear into the silent transparency of the pool. I couldn't remember how I got back down the ladder.

Now, I was at the very edge of that board, trembling in amazed unison with its springiness. From behind me came a rising chorus of impatience chanted by unknown children waiting their turn to dive or jump; they were cruelly unconcerned with my plight. "Chicken, yellow, fairy, jump. Fairy, fairy, jump." From below, I heard the voice of my father intoning, "you don't have to jump, come back down. You don't have to jump."

Why had I climbed the ladder? Some unformed urge to get away from my father embroiled with an even more amorphous urge to win his approval stormed through my head. "You fairy don't have to jump, yellow, jump, don't jump, chicken, yellow fairy." I clamped my eyes closed and found myself again engulfed by the furious flames that had surrounded me and my brother, the previous week in the local movie theater. Now, hiss and crackle was all I could hear.

A whole week had passed since I had seen my first movie; but ceaselessly and unbeckoned it still flickered through my mind, in sleep and in wakefulness. I never went anywhere with my brother, almost never even saw him. Only a year separated us, but we seldom spoke and never played together. Even, at the dinner table, I was all but unaware of his presence. Then, my mother, as a special treat, had sent us to the neighboring village to see our first movie. My brother sneered at the need to go with me. Sneer turned to incredulous disgust when he saw that his unwanted younger brother had been so enthralled and terrified by the conflagration that roared through the final battle of the movie they had been sent to, that he had involuntarily wet his pants and soaked his theater seat. My brother dragged me out before the story ended and before my pissing could turn into a public outcry. "It's only make-believe, you jerk."

For months to come that fire would threaten my daily retreat with the growing cast of characters I met in the art books my mother had belatedly unpacked and arranged in the bookshelf that rose like a bastion to guard the Oriental carpet's border. The new recruits were mostly of Italian origin; my favorite amongst them was Botticelli's Zephyr, whose embodiment of gentle wind animated a verdant tapestry of Spring, even more radiant than that of the carpet.

I never felt alone, but I was always separate. I had many dreams but very few memories. My brother had many friends and fought many fights with those who wanted him to be a German, in their war games. From my brother, I first heard the word Nazi. "I don't want to be a German, I don't want to be a Nazi," my brother would yell at my uncomprehending grandmother. I, myself, refused all confrontation. I always stood in silence until I all but disappeared, and then went about doing what I had initially set out to do. In this way, I seldom failed to get what I wanted.

No one had called me a Nazi. My mother had, for a long time, refused to explain this epithet to me. But, then, the gnarled old woman across the hall took to lurking behind her door, waiting for someone to leave our apartment, so she and her door could creak open and snarl, "Nazi." So persistent was her snarling "Nazi" that my mother relented in her refusal to explain the meaning of the word. My grandmother, one day, threw a full basket of her carefully harvested vegetables at the old crone; but I chose never to hear her and refused even to raise my eyes to the malignance of her curse.

More truly terrifying had been the hissing black vipers that surrounded my bed with their venom and threatened me with never seeing my mother or father again. For many months, I had been sick; one childhood disease after another was poured into the ever hotter cauldron of my body. Chicken pox, measles, mumps, and then the scratchy rage of whooping cough; each, in turn, left its mark. Regardless of the doctor's varying prescriptions, my grandmother treated each new sickness the same, tightly binding my chest with poultices and invoking the healing power of sweat. I drifted in and out of a mild, not unpleasant, delirium often accompanied by the disembodied voices of the radio that was posted by my bedside. The Green Hornet, Stella Dallas, Lorenzo Jones, and various biblical characters from *The Greatest Story Ever Told* brought an almost bearable rhythm to my bondage. But then I was taken to a hospital to have my tonsils removed and was quickly surrounded by black-hooded and hissing nuns whose sternness not even my grandmother could have acted out. "There is no ice-cream for you; you don't deserve it. You must pray, you have to eat your pabulum. If you don't eat your pabulum, you'll never see your mother or your father again."

At first this alien black-robed tribe seemed like some punishment sent to exorcise the sins of the furtive play I had indulged in under the sheets of my sickbed. Involuntarily my hand had started to seek out my penis, when no one was in the room, other than the voices of my radio companions. I thought I heard Tad, as I pulled back my foreskin and started to massage my hardness. Very quickly my apprehension dissolved in the splendid itch of an erection. Only the thought of my grandmother could wither my pleasure. Sometimes an erection called to my hand spontaneously, when my room was filled with people, and forced me to push it between my legs and writhe uncomfortably until it returned to limpness. Sometimes it woke me out of sound sleep and called quickly for my hand, while my eyes still sought to part the darkness. It seemed to have a mind and a body of its own, attached to but separate from my own. I thought of it as "it" and slowly endowed it with a personality; but still it remained a mystery.

I was sure the nuns were seeking retribution. They might even find a tailor with big scissors to enact their raving threats. It was hard to believe that so much anger could be focused on a bowl of pabulum. "Eat your pabulum. If you can't pray, at least eat your pabulum." One of the nuns tried to force a spoonful into my mouth. My teeth clamped into defiant closure. Another nun tried to force open my lower jaw. "I hate pabulum, my father's gone," I spewed out with such vehemence that the spoonful of pabulum splattered on one of the nun's habits, threatening its starched blackness with unruly, sticky viscosity. Her face raged into mine and spat back, "You'll never see your mother again," and slapped me hard. In chorus, they all glided out, ignoring my final "I hate pabulum."

They were all behind me, all of them hissing, chanting, cursing, sneering, taunting. "Nazi, fairy, yellow, jump, pabulum, never, chicken, see, jump, don't jump, your mother again." I opened my eyes. The voices ceased momentarily. I knew I would always be scared of heights. I didn't jump. I dived. My legs went out over my head; my back smashed painfully into the water but didn't break. The water still welcomed me and enveloped my body in a whoosh of lavish silence. My hands were greeted by the bottom of the pool; I stretched my body into horizontality and swam the length of the pool, underwater, knowing people would be wondering why I hadn't surfaced under the diving board and maybe worrying that I might have hurt myself. I wished I could stay underwater longer. When I came up, at the shallow end of the pool, I couldn't see my father.